THE GRAND
INQUISITOR

FYODOR DOSTOEVSKY

THE GRAND INQUISITOR

with related chapters from
THE BROTHERS KARAMAZOV

Edited, with an Introduction, by
CHARLES B. GUIGNON

Translated by
CONSTANCE GARNETT

Hackett Publishing Company
Indianapolis/Cambridge

99   98   97   96   95   94   93   1   2   3   4   5   6   7

Text design by Dan Kirklin

For further information, please address

Hackett Publishing Company, Inc.
P.O. Box 44937
Indianapolis, Indiana 46244-0937

Library of Congress Cataloging-in-Publication Data
Dostoyevsky, Fyodor, 1821–1881.
    [Brat'ia Karamazovy. English. Selections]
    The Grand Inquisitor: with related chapters from The Brothers
Karamazov/Fyodor Dostoevsky: edited and introduced by Charles B.
Guignon; translated by Constance Garnett.
      p.   cm.
    Contents: Grand Inquisitor—Russian Monk.
    ISBN 0-87220-228-3 (cloth)   ISBN 0-87220-193-7 (pbk.)
    I. Guignon, Charles B., 1944–   . II. Garnett, Constance Black,
1862–1946. III. Title.
PG3326.B7E5 1993   93-28077
891.73 ' 3—dc20   CIP

Contents

The Grand Inquisitor

Book V   Pro and Contra

Book VI   The Russian Monk

A Note on the Translation

The Constance Garnett translation of *The Brothers Karamazov*, first published in 1912, has been so widely used over the years that it has become a classic in its own right. Scholars generally agree that Garnett does a remarkable job of capturing Dostoevsky's meaning, even if she occasionally fails to capture his unique style.

For this edition, a few minor changes to the translation have been made, mainly in order to update the vocabulary and style. But Garnett's use of "man" and "mankind" has been retained, in part because it is characteristic of the writing of the late nineteenth century, even though such usage sounds sexist by today's standards.

Introduction

"*The Brothers Karamazov* is the most magnificent novel ever written: the episode of the Grand Inquisitor, one of the peaks in the literature of the world, can hardly be valued too highly." So wrote Sigmund Freud in 1928.[1] And though the novel has had its critics (most notably D. H. Lawrence and Vladimir Nabokov), a number of influential thinkers in our century have shared Freud's opinion. The philosopher Ludwig Wittgenstein is said to have read *The Brothers Karamazov* "so often he knew whole passages of it by heart, particularly the speeches of the elder Zossima, who represented for him a powerful Christian ideal, a holy man who could 'see directly into the souls of other people.'"[2] Martin Heidegger, the seminal figure of existentialism, identified Dostoevsky's thought as one of the most important sources for his early work, *Being and Time* (1929).[3] And, by the middle of the twentieth century, the novel's most fascinating character, Ivan Karamazov, had become the icon of existentialist rebellion in the writings of Albert Camus and Jean-Paul Sartre.

Dostoevsky's insights into the Russian spirit have been confirmed by the history of the Soviet Union. Written in 1879, long before the events of 1905 and 1917, *The Brothers Karamazov* describes the conditions that were to lead to revolution in Russia: the rich, Dostoevsky writes, "live only for mutual envy, for luxury and ostentation, . . . while the poor drown their unsatisfied need and their envy in drunkenness. But soon they will drink blood instead of wine, they are being led on to it." And there is also a premonition of why the revolution will eventually fail: "The salvation of Russia comes from the people. . . . An unbelieving reformer will never do anything in Russia, even if he

1. "Dostoevsky and Parricide," reprinted in *Dostoevsky: A Collection of Critical Essays,* ed. René Wellek (Englewood Cliffs, N.J.: Prentice Hall, 1962), p. 98, quoted in Robin Feuer Miller, *The Brothers Karamazov: Worlds of the Novel* (New York: Twayne, 1992), p. 5.
2. Ray Monk, *Ludwig Wittgenstein: The Duty of Genius* (New York: Penguin, 1990), p. 136. Monk points out that *The Brothers Karamazov* was among the few possessions Wittgenstein brought with him to the front during World War I.
3. Martin Heidegger, *Frühe Schriften* (Frankfurt am Main: Klostermann, 1972), p. x. Of the two portraits Heidegger kept on the wall of his office, one was of Dostoevsky.

is sincere in heart and a genius. Remember that! The people will meet the atheist and overcome him, and Russia will be one and orthodox."

The Brothers Karamazov is above all a novel of ideas. We know that Dostoevsky regarded Books V and VI—including "Rebellion," "The Grand Inquisitor," and "The Russian Monk"—as the "culminating point" of the work.[4] The Grand Inquisitor legend especially has proved to be captivating to readers over the years, so much so that it frequently has been excerpted from the novel and published as an independent piece. It would be a serious mistake, however, to regard the Grand Inquisitor story as stating Dostoevsky's own views in any way. Dostoevsky made it quite clear that he regarded the passages titled "Rebellion" and "The Grand Inquisitor" as "expressions of atheism," reflections of the viewpoint of the "atheist" and "anarchist," Ivan Karamazov, which he hoped to *refute* in the following book, "The Russian Monk." Though Ivan's stance echoes beliefs Dostoevsky held in his younger days, results of what he called the "crucible of doubt" he passed through on his way to faith, it is clear that Dostoevsky opposed these views by the time he wrote *The Brothers Karamazov.* He expresses worries in his letters about whether in the following chapters, the account of the sayings and life of Father Zossima, he will succeed in refuting the "negative" impression left by Ivan's diatribe:

> As an answer to all this *negative side,* I am offering this sixth book, "A Russian Monk." . . . And I tremble for it in this sense: will it be a *sufficient* answer? All the more so because *the answer here is not a direct one, it is not a point-by-point response to any previously expressed positions* (in the Grand Inquisitor or earlier) but only an oblique response . . . so to speak, in an *artistic picture.*[5]

We can see why it is wrong to tear the Inquisitor story out of context if we understand Dostoevsky's method in *The Brothers Karamazov.* Instead of simply presenting his own views, as one might in a philosophical tract, Dostoevsky's approach is to create characters who em-

4. See Nathan Rosen, "Style and Structure in *The Brothers Karamazov* (The Grand Inquisitor and the Russian Monk)," reprinted in *The Brothers Karamazov: A Norton Critical Edition,* ed. Ralph E. Matlaw (New York: Norton, 1976): 841–51.

5. *Pis'ma,* IV, p. 209, Aug. 24/Sept. 13, 1879, quoted in Mikhail Bakhtin, *Problems of Dostoevsky's Poetics,* trans. Caryl Emerson (Minneapolis: University of Minnesota Press, 1984), p. 97, translation modified.

body specific worldviews or orientations, and then to play them off against one another in the action of the novel. For this reason it is important to pay attention to *who* formulates the different positions that appear in the book. The Grand Inquisitor legend is a story cooked up by the Westernized intellectual, Ivan, and it is presented in the context of a discussion with his younger brother, the naive novice monk Alyosha. It is a response to Alyosha's earlier remarks (in the chapter called "Rebellion"), and it is the springboard for "The Russian Monk" that follows it.

Dostoevsky's procedure here is an example of what Mikhail Bakhtin has identified as the new art form created by Dostoevsky: the polyphonic novel. Where traditional novels are monological or homophonic, presupposing a single worldview and moving toward a final synthesis of opposing views, a polyphonic novel creates a set of characters, each endowed with a distinctive voice and worldview, who are pitted against one another in an open-ended dialogue. In a polyphonic novel, according to Bakhtin, there is a "plurality of independent and unmerged voices and consciousnesses, a genuine polyphony of fully valid voices."[6] In such a novel, any character's point of view is "from the beginning a *rejoinder* in an unfinished dialogue."[7] Thoughts and statements appear as reflections of points of view in a space of oppositions; they make sense only within "a world of consciousnesses mutually illuminating one another, a world of yoked-together semantic orientations."[8] For this reason there is no room for an authoritative authorial voice in a Dostoevsky novel. Such a voice would enter "the artistic context as an alien body"; there would be "no space around it to play in, no contradictory emotions"; it would not be "surrounded by an agitated and cacophonous dialogic life."[9]

It is only in the "agitated and cacophonous" space of dialogic exchange, then, that Dostoevsky's ideas take shape. Ivan's Grand Inquisitor story, far from presenting Dostoevsky's own views, must be understood as an expression of Ivan's "atheistic" outlook whose meaning depends on its place in the to and fro of Ivan's interchange with

6. Bakhtin, *Problems of Dostoevsky's Poetics*, pp. 6–7, italics removed.
7. Ibid., p. 32.
8. Ibid., p. 97.
9. Bakhtin, "Discourse in the Novel," in *The Dialogic Imagination*, ed. Michael Holquist (Austin: The University of Texas Press, 1981), p. 344, quoted in Malcolm V. Jones, *Dostoyevsky after Bakhtin: Readings in Dostoyevsky's Fantastic Realism* (Cambridge: Cambridge University Press, 1990), p. 167.

his younger brother. But it would be going too far to suggest that Dostoevsky never gives us a hint of his own views. As he indicated at the time, the words of Zossima in "The Russian Monk" come very close to his own beliefs: "I fully share the thoughts [Zossima] expresses," he wrote, though "if I were to express them myself, *in my own voice*, I would do so in another language and in another form."[10] But the deep response to Ivan's stance is found not so much in the words of any character as in the actual events of the novel. Dostoevsky is not content simply to say what is wrong with Ivan's stance—indeed, he thinks that, within Ivan's rationalist worldview, his views are "irrefutable." Instead, he *shows* the inadequacy of Ivan's stance by displaying its destructive existential implications in the actions and interactions of the characters throughout the novel as a whole.

In Dostoevsky's view, the only way to answer philosophical and theological doubts is by drawing on and making manifest the deep understanding of life embodied in our active lives. The questions he asks are: What are the existential consequences of a particular ideology? What form of life follows from this way of thinking? How will such a viewpoint pan out in action? For what is important to Dostoevsky is not whether propositions are true or false in some abstract sense, but whether the form of life they embody and express is *viable* or not. And that is something we can find out only by unfolding a cogent narrative of the lives of those who instantiate particular worldviews. Thus, the full "refutation" of Ivan's stance only emerges in the unfolding story of his life and of the lives of those who refuse to accept his worldview.

The action of *The Brothers Karamazov* is set in the 1860s, a time of tremendous turmoil and upheaval in Russia. In trying to understand Dostoevsky's vision of the events in Russia, it is important to see that the transition from feudalist to Enlightenment beliefs, which had occurred gradually over centuries in Western Europe, took place suddenly in Russia in the space of a few decades.

The result was a wrenching shift in Russian life, a transformation resulting from the sudden influx of Western European ideologies into a soil not at all prepared for them. The abolition of serfdom in 1861,

10. Quoted in Miller, *The Brothers Karamazov: World of the Novel*, p. 73.

initially embraced with joy by social reformers, quickly turned into a nightmare for both peasants and landed gentry. Required to pay restitution for their emancipation, the peasants sank into debt and servitude, while the gentry lost its lands to the new class of capitalists. Though Dostoevsky originally had supported the reforms, he now felt they were doomed to failure, for they resulted from the contamination of indigenous Russian life with liberal European ideals and institutions quite alien to the Russian spirit. With characteristic indirectness he puts his own views into the mouth of the long-winded prosecutor at the end of the novel: "Reforms, when the ground has not been prepared for them, especially if they are institutions copied from abroad, do nothing but mischief."

Much of *The Brothers Karamazov* is a polemic against the different intellectual movements behind these reforms. There were two waves of reform-minded intelligentsia in the mid-nineteenth century, aptly referred to by Turgenev as the "fathers" and the "sons." The older generation consisted of the Social Romantics of the 1840s, mostly liberal gentry influenced by French Utopian Socialism, German Idealism, and the glorification of the individual in Romantic literature. Drawing their inspiration from abroad, these reformers promised to bring about universal harmony and happiness on earth by applying scientific theories in re-engineering society. As a matter of fact, however, it was not so much science as Christian philanthropic ideals of achieving heaven on earth that informed their vision.

The younger generation of the 1860s were contemptuous of the sentimental Romantic idealism of the 1840s generation. Regarding the older reformers as half-hearted and dishonest, they insisted on carrying the insights of Western science through to their logical conclusions. If it is true, as science tells us, that all people are motivated solely by self-interest, and if it is true that all events result from material causes determined by the laws of physics, then the older generation's dewy-eyed attachment to brotherly love and the ideals of the social gospel must be maudlin illusions we would do well to cast off. The "new men" of the 1860s, dubbed "Nihilists" by Turgenev, rejected all traditional Christian values and set out to design an ideal society based solely on the principles of mechanistic materialism.

By far and away the most influential statement of this new wave of Utopian socialist reform was Chernyshevsky's 1863 novel, *What Is To Be Done?* It has been said that "since the introduction of printing presses into Russia no printed work has had such a great success in

Russia as Chernyshevsky's *What Is To Be Done?*"[11] Chernyshevsky envisions a community of rationalist-revolutionaries who, strictly following the precepts of rational egoism, act solely out of enlightened self-interest. His claim is that, because clear-sighted self-interest entails the Utilitarian principle of the greatest good for the greatest number, the egoists in this ideal society naturally will act for the good of all. What is important is to expunge all emotional attachments in order to make one's actions "comply with the icy logic of social utility."[12] According to Chernyshevsky's convoluted reasoning, when the heroic "new people" succeed in controlling society, nature will finally be conquered, humans will have achieved the fullest possible autonomy, and human society will be re-structured so that every possible desire is completely satisifed. As the icon for this perfect society based on reason Chernyshevsky took the "Crystal Palace" near London, the glass and steel World's Fair center that had been converted into a museum of industry and science.

As a young man Dostoevsky had supported the liberal movements of the 40s, and he had spent ten years in Siberia for his participation in one of its more extremist circles. His years among the prisoners had revealed to him the deep spirituality and intense commitment to freedom of even the simplest Russian people. The ideal of the Crystal Palace—a world in which freedom, love, and faith are replaced by determinism, egoism, and materialism—struck him as totally alien to the Russian soul. Many of his greatest works after returning to St. Petersburg in 1859 were devoted to refuting the vision of reality of the new generation of reformers, especially of Chernyshevsky.

Dostoevsky's method is immanent critique. Instead of simply criticizing the reformers' views and presenting his own counterposition, he tries to get inside the worldview of the Nihilists, to see things from their point of view, and, by carrying their basic assumptions through to their inevitable existential conclusions, to show the ultimate incoherence of their positions. As Dostoevsky sees it, there is a gap between the explicit claims made by the reformers—the theories and

11. Quoted in Joseph Frank, *Dostoevsky: The Stir of Liberation, 1860–1865* (Princeton: Princeton University Press, 1986), p. 285n. Lenin, who "recalled the work in every slight detail," was enraged if anyone criticized the aesthetic qualities of *What Is to Be Done?*, claiming that Chernyshevsky "*completely transformed my outlook*" (Frank, *ibid.*).

12. Frank, *The Stir of Liberation*, p. 288.

positions they propose—and the actual feelings and motivations underlying their schemes. On the one hand, they claim that they are acting out of unbounded concern for "humanity": the desire to improve the human condition and to bring peace and happiness to earth. Yet, on the other hand, a close look at the intellectuals' stance reveals a quite different motivation. Behind the show of humanitarian love is a craving for *power*, an impulse to stand above the crowd and be like gods.

It is not hard to see how this desire to dominate arises. In Dostoevsky's view, the intelligentsia have severed their ties to their homeland and turned to Western Europe for inspiration. Having detached themselves from the Russian stream of life, they feel isolated, uprooted, homeless. Cut off from others, lacking any sense of connectedness to the larger community, they try to vindicate their misery by conjuring up images of themselves as superior people, benefactors of humankind, martyrs for a higher cause. They want to be recognized by others as martyrs and saints. But in fact their vanity and condescending manner repels ordinary people, and in the end they feel ever more bitter and isolated as they sink deeper and deeper into their own narcissistic self-absorption.

Dostoevsky's claim, then, is that it is a drive toward self-affirmation and self-aggrandizement that motivates the reformers' attempts to transform human society. Compensating for their feelings of being outsiders, they try to prove their superiority and worth by presenting themselves as an elite who will be like gods to the weak and helpless masses. What appears as selfless devotion to others, then, turns out to be pride and egoism.

The reformers' underlying motivation in turn dictates a particular picture of the masses they set out to help. To these proud dispensers of beneficence, the people appear as recipients of charity—as weak creatures, helpless victims of a heartless universe, who are incapable of caring for themselves and so are in need of the ministration and expertise of social engineers. But treating people as objects of pity obviously tends to degrade people, relegating them to the status of *things* on hand to be manipulated rather than as potential creators who are capable of taking charge of their own lives. Pity here is a façade for contempt. As Dostoevsky put it in his notes for the Grand Inquisitor legend: "A second Tower of Babel stands in the place of the high ideals created by Christ. The sublime Christian view of human nature sinks down to the view of an animal herd and, under the banner of Social Love, shows entirely unconcealed its contempt for mankind."[13]

Dostoevsky regards the reformers' idealism as misdirected religious enthusiasm—worthy Christian philanthropic ideals twisted into secular humanist ends. One of the wisest characters in the novel says that "even those who have renounced Christianity and attack it in their innermost being still follow the Christian idea," for no one "has been able to create a higher ideal of humanity and of virtue" than that formulated centuries ago. By stripping these ideals from their spiritual context, however, the social reformers debase them and rob them of their power. Renouncing Christ, alienated from the springs of Russian life, the reformers try to put themselves in the place of God, and in doing so only succeed in undermining the people's faith and capacity for love.

Dostoevsky was active in a movement called the *pochvennichestvo* (from the word *pochva* meaning "native soil," but also "ground" or "foundation") which tried to counteract the Westernizing influences seeping into Russia by grounding reforms in the indigenous practices and beliefs of the Russian people.[14] The novel's constant references to "Mother Earth," to falling on the earth and to kissing the earth, convey this imagery of connectedness to the native soil and to the ground of one's existence. In Dostoevsky's view, only if reform starts from the concrete forms of life of Russia itself could it hope to achieve meaningful and lasting change. From this perspective, the attempt to design a new society from scratch, using only scientific principles as revealed to detached rationality, must fail.

"The Grand Inquisitor" and Dostoevsky's response appear approximately a third of the way into *The Brothers Karamazov*. The preceding pages introduce the main characters and develop the tensions that make up the main plot: the murder and the attempt to identify the killer. The actions of the book's central characters—the father, Fyodor, and the three brothers, Alyosha, Dmitri, and Ivan—make manifest Dostoevsky's view of human nature and the different existential stances it makes possible.

13. Quoted in Ellis Sandoz, *Political Apocalypse: A Study of Dostoevsky's Grand Inquisitor* (Baton Rouge: Louisiana State University Press, 1971), pp. 79–80.
14. Frank, *The Stir of Liberation*, pp. 34–47.

The nominal hero of *The Brothers Karamazov*, Alyosha, is initially one of the less interesting characters in the book. A deeply religious novice monk, somewhat childlike and effete, he spends most of his time in the first third of the novel rushing from one character to another trying to be helpful. Though others call him an "angel" and seek his company, his presence often only seems to make things worse. There are hints that there is a deep turmoil in Alyosha's heart that will eventually rise to the surface. One character remarks, "You're a quiet one, Alyosha, you're a saint, I know . . . but you've been down to the depths. . . . You're a Karamazov yourself. . . . You're a sensualist from your father, a crazy saint from your mother." At the outset of the novel the narrator tells us that *The Brothers Karamazov* is only a preliminary to his main story. This main story is most likely a book Dostoevsky planned, called *The Life of a Great Sinner*, which would trace Alyosha's path through sin and despair to final redemption. That Alyosha seems so pallid in *The Brothers Karamazov* shows Dostoevsky's belief that it is only by passing through the dark night of the soul and embracing suffering that one can come into God's grace and so become fully human.

Where Alyosha is often little more than a spectator to the book's events, the other characters present strong images of possible existential stances. Fyodor Karamazov is described as a "sensualist." A buffoon and a profligate, he is driven by lust, endlessly pursuing carnal pleasures and acting impulsively. Through a shrewd business sense and an inheritance from his deceased wife he has become quite wealthy and so can buy the favors of a beautiful young woman named Grushenka. Fyodor's raw sensuality provides the model for what throughout the book is called "the Karamazov": "a crude, unbridled, earthly force," the source of animalistic drives and passions, which has much in common with what Freud later called the id. This earthy "Karamazov" force embodies the dark drives and desires that lead to brutality and destructiveness, but it is also the source of the "will to live," the "thirst for life" that makes one cling to life despite its tribulations. One of the great questions in the background of *The Brothers Karamazov* is how to come to terms with this primitive, sensual dimension of human existence.

Dmitri Karamazov (or Mitya), the oldest of the brothers and the pivotal figure in the book's main action, seems very much like his father. Before the main action of the novel, he had become betrothed to an aristocratic young woman, Katrina Ivanova, by exploiting a family crisis in her life. Hearing of her desperate need for money to save her father's honor, Dmitri offered to give Katrina a large sum of money if she would come to his chambers "secretly." In desperation and shame, Katrina subjected herself to this humiliating act. When she appeared in his chambers, however, Dmitri (who had just received six thousand rubles from his father as a final settlement of his inheritance) resisted the temptation to take advantage of her and instead simply presented her with five thousand rubles. Feeling shamed and indebted, the proud Katrina responds by vowing her eternal love to Dmitri. But Dmitri in the meantime has fallen for Grushenka's charms and, when Katrina entrusts three thousand rubles to his safe-keeping, he shamelessly takes off on a wild jaunt with Grushenka and apparently squanders the entire amount in one weekend. The tensions of the plot are in place as Katrina, now finding herself in love with Ivan, spitefully clings to Dmitri to avenge her wounded honor, while Dmitri finds himself in a bitter struggle with his father for the love of Grushenka.

The main contours of Dostoevsky's view of human nature are laid out in a heartfelt confession of Dmitri to Alyosha. For Dostoevsky, humans are made up of two conflicting dimensions or two conflicting sets of needs. On the one hand, there is the earthy, sensualist side of the self, the "Karamazov" dimension of raw, amoral cravings and dark desires. This aspect of the self is evident in Dmitri's sense of the overpowering force of his own sensuality and the almost voluptuous delight he gets from seeing the degradation not only of Katrina, but of himself as well. The raw, "primitive force" of the Karamazov is not something Dostoevsky sees as entirely negative. Though it is often referred to with such animal terms as "insect" or "reptile," it is a fundamental part of our creaturely being, and so is an inescapable part of who we are.

In his sensuality Dmitri is very much like his father. But unlike his father, he also feels a different force within himself: the need to rise above his sheer animal nature and achieve something higher. Dostoevsky sees that, unlike lower animals, humans are seldom content with simply satisfying basic needs and being able to survive. It is characteristic of humans that they also feel a need to realize higher, more spiritual ideals. We seek to achieve a better, nobler life than that of mere getting by—a life that can be characterized as courageous or loving or honest.

In other words, we feel a need to *transcend* our mere sensual nature by realizing specifically human aims. This idea is often expressed by saying that humans are not just driven by raw *de facto* desires, for they also care about what *sorts* of desires they have, and so they try to regulate their basic desires according to higher principles. To be human is to care about what sorts of character traits one has; that is why there can be such things as honor among thieves or concern about one's dignity even in abject poverty. In prison Dostoevsky had been struck by how this inbuilt, unreflective craving for something spiritual in one's life could be elicited in even the most hardened criminals by reading to them simple stories from the Bible. In his view, the "idealistic" dimension of the self is just as basic to us as the "sensual," Karamazov side. It explains Dmitri's last-minute restraint when he had the opportunity to take advantage of Katrina, and it now creates his sense of shame for having spent Katrina's money on his excursion with Grushenka.

Dmitri is intensely aware that he is torn apart by these conflicting needs. On the one hand, a true "Karamazov," he takes perverse pleasure in being a hell-bent sensualist: "I'm a Karamazov. For when I leap into the pit, I go headlong with my heels up, and am pleased to be falling in that degrading attitude, and pride myself on it." Yet, on the other hand, he also feels the desire to be a better person: "in the very depths of that degradation," he says, "I begin a hymn of praise." This shattering paradox—being torn between the sensual and the idealistic, able to love both Sodom and the Virgin Mary—defines the human condition. "I can't endure the thought that a man of lofty mind and heart begins with the ideal of the Madonna and ends with the ideal of Sodom. What's still more awful is that a man with the ideal of Sodom in his soul does not renounce the ideal of the Madonna, and in his heart may be on fire with that ideal, genuinely on fire, just as in the days of youth and innocence." Dmitri's struggle between his idealism and his sensuality reflects the central question posed by *The Brothers Karamazov*: Is there any way to reconcile the tension within the self in order to achieve peace and fulfillment in this life? And, as becomes quite clear, this is also the question for the future prospects of Russia itself.

The Brothers Karamazov is at one level a story about the struggle between good and evil.[15] Dostoevsky believed that the capacities for

15. My discussion here draws extensively on a brilliant study of *The Brothers Karamazov* by Charles Taylor which is, sadly, still unpublished.

both good and evil are fundamental to our existence, part of the undercurrent of raw life itself. He had little patience with the Utopian reformers who thought that humans are fundamentally good, and that it is only their upbringing or socialization that causes evil. Seeing evil this way treats it as something "subjective"—as a psychological "problem" that one can "disown" since it is not really one's own. On the view of the liberal reformers, there really is no real evil; there are only dysfunctional families or unfair social conditions. Evil is not something I _do_; it is something that _befalls_ me from outside.

In contrast, Dostoevsky holds that at the core of human nature there is a deep-seated capacity for evil—what we might call "primal evil"—which cannot be explained away in psychological or sociological terms. This "objective" evil is a fundamental and irreducible part of our sensual nature, as much a part of who we are as our love of life and concern for others. Primal evil appears in the almost daily accounts of wanton and pointless viciousness that come to us from around the world—the reports of cruelty, torture, rape, and destruction we find so appalling (yet also somehow fascinating). Dostoevsky kept a collection of newspaper clippings dealing with cases of cruelty to children and animals, and in the chapter called "Rebellion" he has Ivan Karamazov recite a blood-chilling litany of such stories to his brother, Alyosha.

What becomes clear from these stories is how the torturers derive an almost voluptuous sensual pleasure from their brutality: "I know for a fact there are people who at every blow are worked up to sensuality, to literal sensuality, which increases at every blow they inflict. They beat for a minute, for five minutes, for ten minutes, more often and more savagely." This capacity for cruelty appears in the "love of torturing children. . . . It's just their defenselessness that tempts the tormentor, just the angelic confidence of the child who has no refuge and no appeal, that sets his vile blood on fire." Ivan sees that there is an "intoxication of cruelty," a physical thrill that comes from inflicting pain, and that this is not just an aberration found in a few unhinged individuals but is something that runs deeply through all of us. In every man, he says, "a demon lies hidden—the demon of rage, the demon of lustful heat at the screams of the tortured victim, the demon of lawlessness let off the chain. . . ."

Primal evil is evil for its own sake. Though in most of us these cruel and brutal drives are kept under wraps, they are near the surface, ready to bubble up given the slightest opportunity. We see primal evil in the atrocities of the Nazis, in the "dirty wars" in South America, in the killing fields of Cambodia, and, more recently, in the bloodbath in the former Yugoslavia. It is the driving force behind rioting, looting, and burning in the cities, behind "blood sports" and military war games, and behind such "innocent" children's pastimes as dismembering insects or torturing cats. It is at the root of the verbal abuse and subdued violence of domestic life, of the bullying men slip into in their relations with women, and of the sneering sarcasm and point-scoring of academic conversation. Because of this seemingly boundless capacity for raw, unmitigated evil Freud concluded, *Homo homini lupus*, "Man is a wolf to man."[16] Or, as one of the characters in *The Brothers Karamazov* remarks, people "all declare that they hate evil, but secretly they all love it."

The recognition that there is a primal drive to evil within the human soul is hardly unique to Dostoevsky. What is most striking about his view is his understanding of what is necessary to subdue or tame this force. Dostoevsky feels that there is no way to rip out these dark and vicious desires solely through one's own will. For the drive to evil is generally bound up with the sensual, "Karamazov" dimension of the self, and in this sense is fundamental to our creaturely existence: it is part of the groundrhythm of life that also includes such good drives as those of compassion, love, and the will to live. For this reason there is no way for us to disentangle and extricate the dark desires without destroying some of the best things about ourselves in the process.

The Brothers Karamazov presents two unsatisfactory responses to primal evil. The first, found in Fyodor and to some extent in Dmitri, is the response of gleefully embracing the evil, taking an almost masochistic pleasure in one's degradation and self-debasement. The second response, found in Katrina, Ivan, and other more "refined" characters, starts with a reaction of horror and revulsion toward the primal evil in oneself. Recognizing my own capacity for cruelty and being appalled by it, I respond by *recoiling* from the evil within myself, trying to rid myself of it by becoming a purer, more perfect sort of person, untouched by such brutish, undignified tendencies. This desire not to have dirty hands is driven by the "idealistic" dimension of the self, the longing to be a higher, better sort of person. It is the impulse to rise

16. *Civilization and Its Discontents*, trans. James Strachey (New York: Norton, 1989), p. 69.

above one's creatureliness in order to be supremely pure and untainted by any lower, "merely" human needs and drives.

Dostoevsky's claim is that this second response to evil—the fastidious perfectionism that tries to excise all dark drives and capacities—instead of purifying us, actually drives us into an even deeper form of evil: a "second-order evil" that issues from *pride.*

We can see an example of this in Katrina's response to her disgrace at Dmitri's hands. Humiliated by his action, she does not simply lash out at Dmitri in rage. Instead, she tries to portray herself as a saint and a martyr by pretending to herself (and to everyone else) that she is in love with Dmitri and will devote her life to his welfare. All along, of course, her "love" is actually a form of vengeance. Pretending she has higher, nobler feelings in relation to him, she sets herself up as a martyr to a "higher," more spiritual form of love, and by doing so she sets out to make him look like an insensitive brute. She takes pleasure in imagining her own life extinguished for the sake of Dmitri: "And let him see that all my life I will be true to him and the promise I gave him, in spite of his being untrue and betraying me. I will—I will become nothing but a means for his happiness, or—how shall I say?—an instrument, a machine for his happiness, and that for my whole life, my whole life, and that he may see that all his life!" Behind this pretence of noble self-sacrifice, needless to say, is spitefulness and vindictiveness: "He will learn at least that [I am] one who loves him and has sacrificed all her life to him. I will gain my point. . . . I will be a god to whom he can pray—and that at least he owes me for his treachery and for what I suffered yesterday through him." It is not hard to see that this show of selfless devotion is in fact merely a mask for pride and egoism—the desire to be God and to lord it over others, treating them as mere things on hand for one's own self-glorification.

The attempt to rise above one's earthy, sensual nature through this sort of self-denial is called "laceration." The Russian word, *nadryv,* comes from a verb meaning "to strain" (under a heavy load), "to rupture," or "to tear," and it carries with it the connotation of being ripped or torn. Lacerated individuals are torn apart, both within themselves and in their relations to others. As we have seen, laceration originates in a basically noble impulse: horror in the face of the human capacity for evil. Recoiling in disgust from the primal evil in oneself, one tries to rise above such debasing and undignified tendencies by affirming oneself as a transcendent, more spiritual or noble sort of being. But this attempt to achieve a superior position through one's own will power—to rise above the herd—is quite obviously a product of pride. Trying to make oneself look good by making others look bad, laceration leads to subtly manipulative human relations: others are encountered as tools to be used in achieving one's own self-enhancement. What results from laceration, then, is not angelic behavior, but manipulative power plays and airs of superiority that tear us away from others and ultimately tear us apart within our own selves.

There are two main consequences of laceration. First, there is self-dissociation and self-fragmentation as one strives to deny one's own deepest nature in the name of an assumed "higher" motivation. In laceration I treat one dimension of my identity—the sensual component—as a *thing* which is not really part of who I am as a person, as something at my disposal to work over and transform through my own will. This objectification of the self is a form of self-deception—treating part of myself as something I can *disown*—and it leads to a fractured, incoherent self. Agents of laceration are out of touch with their own feelings, torn apart within themselves, intent on hammering themselves into a new shape through their own will power. In its most extreme form, the lacerated individual is totally unhinged, swinging between grandiosity and self-loathing, incapable of coherent action.

Second, laceration leads to fractured social relationships. Driven by idealistic perfectionism, I try to be above all the others, purer and better than everyone else. In order to be secure in my sense of myself as truly exceptional, however, I must succeed in getting others to *recognize* me as a higher sort of person. Yet the grandiosity and narcissistic self-absorption motivating this perfectionism only repels others, with the result that the agent of laceration is torn away from the community and is left isolated and embittered, more concerned than ever with proving his or her superiority.

In its extreme forms, laceration results in sadism and masochism. As an agent of laceration, I will try to prove my status as a superior sort of person by treating the other person as a mere *object*—a thing I can manipulate and control. Sadism arises as part of the attempt to make myself look good by treating the other as something less than human. But such sadism seems to be self-defeating, for as soon as others are relegated to the status of wounded victims, they show their own capacity for deep suffering as humans, and in so doing they seem to threaten my image of myself as the being with the highest, noblest human qualities. So it now appears that the only way I can prove the depth of my own human feelings is to display *my* capacity for suffering. I therefore contrive to make myself look like a victim, claiming that it is the other who is causing me to suffer: "Don't you see what you are doing to me? Don't you see how miserable you are making me?" This sort of masochism is motivated by a desire to affirm my own superiority by portraying the other as an insensitive, subhuman brute. Both these strategies can occur simultaneously in lacerated relationships, as when Katrina tries to make Dmitri suffer by enacting the part of the degraded and shamed victim whom he must "therefore" (by the deranged logic of laceration) look up to as a god.

What lies behind laceration, obviously, is egoism. Springing from a desire to free oneself from the sensual (and potentially evil) dimension of human existence, one is intent on becoming a self-defining, masterful self—an autonomous individual freed from all "lower" sorts of motivations. But even though laceration seems to originate from an idealistic impulse, it is in fact motivated by vanity and pride—the desire to be more than human, to be "like a god"—and it consequently generates an even more vicious form of second-order evil. Caught in self-deception and grandiosity, bent on being recognized as a superior being, the lacerated individual swings back and forth between dominating others and enacting the part of the wounded victim. This struggle for self-affirmation, far from making one a better person, alienates others, and in the end breeds the feelings of emptiness and worthlessness that lead to even greater forms of cruelty and destructiveness.

The best way to understand "Rebellion" and "The Grand Inquisitor," I believe, is to see them as expressions of Ivan's highly intellectualized form of laceration. In many ways Ivan is the most appealing of the brothers. The only one of the three brothers who has gone to a university, he is an intellectual with a broad knowledge of Western philosophy and science. In the tavern where he meets Alyosha, he speaks of his deep love for the early European scientists, their "passionate faith in their work, their truth, their struggle, and their science." His outrage in the face of reports about atrocities against innocent children shows the depth of his commitment to the Enlightenment ideals of justice and human happiness. In true Enlightenment fashion, he courageously insists on facing up to the facts, and he rejects facile explanations that conceal the reality of what is happening in the world. His newspaper column, called "Eye Witness," suggests the Enlightenment ideal of the detached, dispassionate spectator objectively and impartially reporting on the facts. In his unsentimental, clear-eyed insistence on following ideas through to their logical conclusions, he has much in common with the reformers of the 1860s. But at the same time we find in him an almost child-like love for life. "I have a longing for life, and I go on living in spite of logic," he admits; it is "not a matter of intellect or logic; it's loving with one's inside, with one's stomach."

Nevertheless, there is a dark side to Ivan's character. He makes it clear that his gut-level love for life—this "unseemly [literally, "obscene"] thirst for life"—is something he finds intolerable. And it is not hard to see why. Ivan regards the love of life as a manifestation of the "Karamazov" within himself, the primitive life-force that is also the source of our capacity for primal evil. To accept life, then, is to condone a scheme of things in which there is evil, and so it makes one an *accomplice* in the suffering in the world. Ivan therefore strives to detach himself from his sensual side, to distance it from himself by treating it as something "other" to who he is. Intent on affirming his identity as a pure, transcendent being, he identifies himself solely with his idealistic side and disowns his own creatureliness. And since this means severing his ties to worldly concerns, he resolves not to get entangled in his family's affairs.

There are two ways Ivan's perfectionism shows up in his behavior. First, he attempts to affirm his own identity as something "higher," as an autonomous, self-defining subject. He does this by trying to peel away all his local, merely sentimental attachments in order to achieve the stance of a purely objective and rational observer. This is the Enlightenment dream of achieving a "God's-eye view" or a "view from nowhere"—the ability to see things *sub specie aeternitatis*, unaffected by any narrow attitudes or comforting illusions. Like the early scientists he so admires, Ivan insists on clear-sightedly facing up to the cold, hard "facts" and accepting the implications of his beliefs, no matter what the cost. As it is summed up later in the novel, his philosophy is *"Je pense, donc je suis,"* Descartes's solipsistic, self-congratulatory view of himself as a self-defining, dimensionless point of pure subjectivity. In Ivan's respect for science and in his ironic, dispassionate attitude toward every topic of conversation, we see his quest for rational distance and self-mastery.

Second, Ivan's sense of indignation over the suffering of children and his unwavering commitment to justice and happiness for all display his dedication to the most elevated principles and ideals. This high-minded stance is connected to his determination to be morally flawless. He refuses to act in any way unless his action is justifiable in terms of universally valid moral principles. This is why he finds it "obscene" that the Karamazov in him makes him want to go on living "in spite of logic."

Dostoevsky's claim is that Ivan's stance is untenable, and he develops this diagnosis through a critique of the Western Enlightenment. The Enlightenment starts out from a deep commitment to achieving universal peace and justice. The source of misery and injustice, it holds, is ignorance and confusion. According to the paradigmatic Enlightenment figure, the Baron d'Holbach, "man is unhappy because he has an erroneous view of nature." What is necessary, then, is to arrive at a clear-sighted understanding of reality by adopting a rigorously detached and objective stance toward things. Thus, d'Holbach equates the *loix du monde physique et du monde morale* in the subtitle of his *System of Nature,* expressing the Enlightenment's conviction that objective knowledge of the laws of nature will also reveal to us the truths concerning how we ought to live.[17]

It is a historical fact, however, that this Enlightenment project of achieving human well-being through greater knowledge tended to undermine itself. The initial motivation for scientific objectivity was the dream of bringing about universal peace, justice, and happiness by extinguishing the narrow, parochial attachments that sustain illusion and prejudice. Yet, as this quest for knowledge unfolded, the discoveries made by modern science tended toward a mechanistic and materialistic picture of reality as a vast aggregate of brute, meaningless material objects in causal interactions. Given this mechanized and objectified worldview, however, it becomes increasingly difficult to see why one should be committed to the values that initially motivated the Enlightenment. For if nothing exists except inherently valueless material objects in push-pull causal interactions, it becomes plausible to suppose that values are not part of the furniture of the world, but are instead merely subjective projections of human wishes and longings onto things. Values seem to be made rather than found.

---

17. Quoted from Jürgen Habermas, *Theory and Practice,* trans. John Viertel (Boston: Beacon, 1973), pp. 256, 258.

We might call this the Enlightenment paradox. The Enlightenment started out from the ideal of realizing paradise on earth through the discovery of objective truth. Yet this quest for truth tended to undermine the evaluative commitments that motivated the Enlightenment project in the first place. As a result, the eighteenth-century Enlightenment idealists with their noble ideals (mirrored in the 1840s reformers in Russia) were eventually replaced by the cold, hard-headed materialists of the nineteenth-century "Radical Enlightenment" (mirrored in the 1860s radicals in Russia). Thus, the Enlightenment seems to be self-defeating: when its premises are carried through to their logical conclusions, it ends up undermining its own initial motivations.

The Enlightenment paradox is reflected in Ivan's existential stance. On the one hand, Ivan's humanitarian motives express the noblest ideals and values of Western liberalism. He follows the Enlightenment injunction to remain detached from the affairs of everyday life—to "wear the world like a loose cloak"—in order to stay aligned with the highest principles of justice and benevolence. On the other hand, as we have seen, there is a dark side to Ivan. He confesses to Alyosha that he "could never understand how one can love one's neighbors. . . . To my thinking, Christ-like love for men is a miracle impossible on earth." Ironically, he suspects that anyone who cares for the sick and dying must be guilty of "laceration," of adopting a pose in order to be seen as capable of Christ-like love. But Ivan's inability to understand Christ-like love merely shows that the Enlightenment stance of detached, moral superiority tends to cut us off from the sources of compassion and selfless love that make genuine benevolence possible in the first place. When we become detached, the world, so to speak, goes dead for us: things show up only as brute, meaningless objects on hand for our use. From such a stance, however, nothing really can *matter* to us any longer. The world seems anonymous; nothing *speaks* to us. In the end, meaningful agency becomes impossible. The kind of selfless love possible for all humankind becomes unintelligible to Ivan.

The outcome of Ivan's perfectionist ethic, then, is impotence and paralysis. He wants to be innocent, to keep his hands clean, and in order to achieve this moral superiority he refuses to act until he is sure that action is justified by the highest principles. "Am I my brother's keeper?" he asks, echoing Cain's words. Yet, as the events in the novel show, his refusal to be involved, far from preserving his innocence, in the end incites others to evil actions. Instead of being innocent, he turns out to be most culpable of all.

Ivan is a victim of his own lacerated stance. He finds himself caught up in the groundswell of life, riding its currents with youthful enthusiasm. But he also thinks this will to live cannot be rationally justified. In his effort to disown his gut-level love for life, he becomes a fractured self who is incapable of any sort of coherent action. The only option that makes sense to him is suicide: when his youthful enthusiasm runs out (at the age of thirty), he will "return his ticket."

Dostoevsky's diagnosis of Ivan's existential stance casts light on his view of the West in general. Having drawn its ideals from the Judeo-Christian heritage, Western civilization from the outset embodied the finest vision of life possible for humans. The Enlightenment grew out of this heritage, but insofar as it tried to ground its moral ideals in reason rather than in faith, it tore those ideals out of the context in which they first emerged and made sense. What Dostoevsky wants us to see is that when these values are taken out of their original context, they lose their power to speak to us. As a result, secular reformers tend to undermine their own highest aims. Their idealism is motivated by a determination to rise above the "merely" human with its inherent capacity for evil. But insofar as our capacity for love and compassion in inseparably bound up with the earthy, sensual side of the self, the reformers cut themselves off from the resources that make genuine social feeling possible. Motivated by pride and laceration, incapable of genuine love, they end up being simply on a power trip.

Ivan plays with a theory that Dostoevsky regarded as the inevitable outcome of the perfectionist stance of detachment and moral superiority: the idea that, for higher people, "everything is lawful." If there is no immortality—if "God is dead" and there will be no divine reward or retribution—then why not step outside the law and do whatever you want? From this standpoint, morality looks like a sucker's game. Ivan's deepest thoughts become apparent toward the end of the book: "As soon as men have all of them denied God . . . everything will begin anew." Until that happens, however, "everyone who recognizes the truth even now may legitimately order his life as he pleases, on the new principles. In that sense, 'all things are lawful' for him." The paradox of Ivan's Westernized ideals, then, is that its austere discipline of detachment and self-transformation tends to undermine its own moral underpinnings. In the end this form of idealism spawns a self-serving moral nihilism—as is all too vividly illustrated by the sad history of the Soviet Union.

"Rebellion" and "The Grand Inquisitor" reveal the intellectual underpinnings of Ivan's existential stance. It is important to keep in mind that the ideas developed in these chapters emerge in the course of the discussion between Ivan and Alyosha. Ivan is reaching out to his brother for help, but since he is also bent on shattering his brother's faith, he undermines his chances of being helped. A Westernized intellectual at heart, given to stark dichotomies, Ivan formulates his diatribe in terms of polarized either/or's that leave no room for a third position. Since Alyosha is not equipped to see through this intellectual ploy, the reply to Ivan does not appear until we reach the sayings of the Russian monk.

"Rebellion" presents a variation on the traditional "problem of suffering." The problem gets off the ground if one tries to hold on to three beliefs simultaneously: (1) God is good, (2) God is all-powerful, and (3) there is suffering. The difficulty is obvious. If God is all-powerful and He nevertheless allows suffering, then it is hard to see how He could be good. But if God is truly good and suffering occurs, then it is hard to see how He could be all-powerful. It seems, then, that one of the three beliefs has to be abandoned.

The problem of suffering is as old as the Book of Job, and traditional attempts to solve it generally proceed by denying the third proposition, "There is suffering." Thus, it is said that the suffering that exists is really very insignificant compared to the rewards promised in the after-life, or that a bit of suffering builds character, or that a little suffering is a small price to pay for human freedom. With cold precision Ivan knocks down some of these traditional answers. If suffering exists because "the sins of the fathers are visited on the sons," then God is clearly unjust. If it is claimed that God's form of justice is beyond human comprehension, then it seems to follow that either torture is sometimes good or the word "good" has totally lost its meaning. If the promised after-life is supposed to make up for suffering, then it would appear that divine justice holds that it is all right to torture children provided you give them some candy afterwards. Ivan courageously rejects all these facile "solutions" and insists on sticking to the facts.

But Ivan's intention is not simply to rehash an old puzzle about divine justice. In fact, the position he presents is much more shattering. For Ivan sets up a perfect "no win" situation in which, whether you believe in God or not, the upshot is that there is no way you can justify living in a world where there is such suffering. The problem is therefore not so much that of theodicy (trying to justify the ways of God to humans) as cosmodicy (justifying life in the world). The problem of suffering therefore articulates Ivan's reasons for his decision to commit suicide.

Briefly put, the issue is this. Either God exists or He does not exist. If God exists and permits such awful suffering, then God is cruel, there is no justice in the universe, and life is intolerable. As Ivan says, "It's not that I don't accept God, you must understand, it's the world created by Him I don't and cannot accept." Even if suffering is necessary for the future harmony, harmony is not worth such a price.

Alternatively, if God does not exist, then the picture of the universe formulated by mechanistic materialism must be true. But, in this case, given the point of view of modern science (what Ivan calls "Euclidean reason"), the universe consists of nothing but meaningless material objects in causal interaction, effect follows cause according to the laws of physics, people are determined to do what they do, no one is guilty of anything, and so there are no such things as right or wrong, good or bad. Or, more precisely, the ideals of justice, goodness, benevolence, dignity, and so on turn out to be purely human inventions, the results of projecting *our* needs and wishes onto brute, meaningless matter, and so they are illusions lacking any basis in the order of things. But, on this option also, Ivan finds life intolerable, for the truth of mechanistic materialism seems to imply that the ideals of realizing perfect justice and well-being on earth are nothing but pipe dreams. In that case, however, there is no reason to go on living. "All I know is that there is suffering and that there are none guilty." But Ivan "can't consent to live by" that.

Given this way of putting the issue, it makes no difference whether one believes in God or not. That is why, even though Ivan is a committed atheist, he is perfectly willing for the sake of argument to accept the truth of all traditional religious doctrines. The point is that we get the same conclusion no matter what we think about God: his argument against the world goes through whether there is a God or not.

Of course, Ivan's claim is not merely that there is no reason to live, but that to go on living is reprehensible, almost criminal. For if we continue to live given this scheme of things, we are in effect *endorsing* a universe that is shot through with injustice and suffering. Under these circumstances, to go on living is to be an *accomplice* in the world's injustice, and so to be partly *guilty* for the misery and pain existing everywhere. For a fastidious perfectionist like Ivan, a "lover of humanity" who is unwilling to compromise on the demand for absolute justice for all, one can avoid guilt only by "returning one's ticket" and exiting from the world. As long as the primitive drive of the "Karamazov" makes him cling to life, however, Ivan decides to remain innocent by refusing to be involved in life. He will not be "his brother's keeper."

Dostoevsky thought that the problem of suffering as formulated by Ivan was "irrefutable." There is no way that, using reason, one can vindicate the world and its suffering. Instead of trying to reply to Ivan's arguments, then, what he does is show through the action of the book that Ivan's stance is not viable.

Ivan hopes to remain pure by severing his ties to life and being a detached observer. This stance is now called "rebellion": it is the defiant rejection of one's human limitations, and it is motivated by a desire to be like God. Defiance is evident in the very way in which Ivan poses the problem. He sets himself up as a judge standing outside the world, unconnected to the affairs of everyday life, who uses reason to determine whether there is any ultimate justification for living. The events of the novel show, however, that this attempt to remain pure and undefiled by standing above the world is in fact the *source* of Ivan's inability to see the possibilities of justice and goodness in life itself. It is precisely his "rebellion" and his attempt to be like God that tears him away from the bedrock of everyday life where the answers to his questions can be found. In the end, his stance of detachment breeds a form of evil as virulent as those Ivan originally hoped to root out.

We can understand the point of the Grand Inquisitor legend only if we pay close attention to how it develops out of the dialogue between Ivan and Alyosha in the preceding chapters.[18] At the conclusion of Ivan's tirade, Alyosha makes a remark that would sound quite sensible to a devout believer, though it totally misses the mark as a response to

18. For my interpretation of "The Grand Inquisitor" I am deeply indebted to H. L. Dreyfus's lectures at Berkeley. Dreyfus is currently preparing a full-length study of *The Brothers Karamazov*.

Ivan's attack on faith. He suggests that the coming of Christ, who "gave his innocent blood for all and everything," resolves the problem of suffering.

Now it should be obvious that this response does not help at all. For since the problem is how God can allow the suffering of innocents, it does not seem that the suffering of one more innocent would make things better. And Ivan seems to take an almost sinister pleasure in hearing this proposed solution: "Ah! the one without sin," he sneers, presumably rubbing his hands together. It is in response to this suggestion that he introduces the Grand Inquisitor story: "Do you know, Alyosha . . . I made a poem about a year ago."

As the context of the story shows, then, the legend emerges as Ivan's reply to Alyosha's claim that the coming of Christ has improved the human condition. That is, the story is a continuation of Ivan's attack on faith, a further expression of his atheism. What Ivan suggests in the story is that, contrary to what Alyosha supposes, Christianity has worsened the human condition by placing intolerable demands on humanity. The point of the legend is that, by holding up two sets of irreconcilable and unattainable ideals, the advent of Christ had done nothing but increase the suffering in the world.

The two conflicting ideals introduced by Christianity are presented in the opposition between the Inquisitor and the figure of Christ in the story. Note that the tale takes place in the sixteenth century, the time of the Protestant Reformation, when a "star like to a torch (that is, to a [new] church) fell on the sources of the waters." What this suggests is that the opposition in the Grand Inquisitor story is not between the Inquisitor, regarded as a sort of Antichrist, and Jesus, who has returned to earth to reiterate his original message. On the contrary, the opposition is between two opposed but equally fundamental interpretations of the significance of Christianity: the Roman Catholic interpretation (represented by the Inquisitor), and the Protestant interpretation (the view imputed to the silent figure of Christ by the Inquisitor). On this reading of Ivan's position, his suggestion is that Christianity has consisted of two main branches that have each put forward different and fundamentally opposed ideals. On the one hand, there are the Roman Catholics, who have been dedicated to achieving happiness and well-being for all. On the other hand, there are the Protestants, who make individual freedom and dignity their central aims.

This opposition between Catholic and Protestant interpretations of

Christianity is apparent in the basic issue laid out in the legend: the conflict between freedom and happiness. The highest aim of Catholics, according to Ivan's story, is the goal of achieving peace and happiness for all in a catholic (that is, universal) Church-state. Dostoevsky regarded French socialism, which had so strongly influenced the 1840s reformers, as merely an extension of this old Catholic ideal of achieving universal happiness: "Present-day French socialism," he wrote in his *Diary of a Writer*, "is nothing but the truest and most direct continuation of the Catholic idea, its fullest, most final realization. . . . "[19] Built into Catholicism and socialism, in Dostoevsky's view, is the assumption that since humans are inherently selfish and necessarily in conflict with one another, universal happiness can be achieved only in a social system in which a few superior individuals exert absolute control over the masses, "uniting all in one unanimous and harmonious ant-heap." In other words, universal happiness and peace can be realized only by re-engineering human society according to a rational blueprint in order to force people to cooperate with one another for their mutual benefit. For socialists this means creating a totalitarian state in which people give up their freedom and subject themselves to the absolute control of a secularized Church hierarchy (the kind of political system institutionalized in the Politburo of the Soviet Union, for example).

At the same time, Christianity has always held up an ideal of human freedom and dignity: the image of each person, in a solitary one-to-one relation to God, responsible for his or her own choices. This ideal of autonomy, basically a Pauline doctrine, was made central to Protestantism through Luther's "religious individualism" with its emphasis on the inner condition of faith and on the role of personal *conscience* in reading and interpreting Scripture. The glorification of freedom that the Grand Inquisitor attributes to Christ is in line with the Protestant emphasis on the individual: "Thou didst desire man's free love, that he should follow thee freely," the Inquisitor says to Christ. "Man must hereafter with free heart decide for himself what is good and what is evil, having only Thy image before him as a guide." Thus, Luther abolished the priesthood and denied the existence of miracles in the contemporary world. As the Inquisitor notes, however, this demand for autonomy places an overwhelming burden on people. They

19. Quoted in Geoffrey C. Kabat, *Ideology and Imagination: The Image of Society in Dostoevsky* (New York: Columbia University Press, 1978), p. 24.

must find faith in the solitude of their own hearts, alone before God, without any worldly intermediaries or supports. Since only a small elect can live without such supports, the harsh demands of Protestantism mean that only an elect will achieve salvation.

When reading the Grand Inquisitor story, it is important to keep in mind that this is *Ivan's* story and presupposes Ivan's extremely polarized, "either/or" way of thinking. Both the Grand Inquisitor and the figure of Christ in the story represent aspects of Ivan's own ideals and aspirations. The Grand Inquisitor, like Ivan, is an atheist who claims to love humanity and, like the 1860s radicals, dreams of achieving paradise on earth through a total reworking of human society on rational principles. The Inquisitor also pictures himself as a "great idealist" who has been willing to live as an ascetic in order to become a superior human being. But, as is the case with Ivan, his protestations of humanitarian love merely mask his deep contempt for the people.

But the glorification of freedom and dignity attributed to Christ also reflect Ivan's deepest ideals. These aims, though imputed to Christ, in fact originate not so much from the Gospels as from Luther's religious individualism, and they were worked over by nineteenth-century liberal Protestant theology into our contemporary humanistic interpretation of Christianity. We know that Dostoevsky was reading Luther at the time he wrote *The Brothers Karamazov,* and that he was concerned to reply to the recent humanistic accounts of the "Life of Jesus" by Ernst Renan and David Friedrich Strauss.[20] The picture of Christ in the story clearly reflects Ivan's Protestant-humanistic reading rather than Dostoevsky's own understanding of Christ. This should be clear from the fact that the words and deeds attributed to Christ are often wrong and at times verge on blasphemy. "Thou didst lift them up and thereby taught them to be proud," says the Grand Inquisitor, yet nothing is further from the Gospels than teaching people to be "proud." It is claimed that Jesus rejected miracle, mystery, and authority and "set the example for doing so," yet it was not Jesus but Luther who rejected miracle and authority. And a devout reader of the Bible like Dostoevsky was surely aware that there is no record anywhere of Jesus kissing anyone, and certainly not "on the lips."

20. Robert L. Belknap, *The Genesis of "The Brothers Karamazov": The Aesthetics, Ideology, and Psychology of Text Making* (Evanston, Ill.: Northwestern University Press, 1990), p. 21. See also Victor Terras, *A Karamazov Companion: Commentary on the Genesis, Language, and Style of Dostoevsky's Novel* (Madison: University of Wisconsin Press, 1981), p. 17.

It should be clear, then, that the Grand Inquisitor story sets up an opposition not between, say, secular reformism and authentic Christianity, but between two aspects of Ivan's own anguished longings and ideals. Ivan rightly sees that his humanitarian aims are rooted in the Christian heritage. But, because he tears them out of the context of faith in which they make sense, he cannot see how these goals can be realized. For it appears that the ideals of happiness and freedom are inconsistent with one another. *Either* we can follow the Catholic dream of happiness and peace for all in a vast totalitarian state, but then we must abandon our desire for freedom and dignity, as people are turned into slaves. *Or* we can accept the Protestant demand of individual freedom and responsibility without wordly supports, but then the vast majority of humanity is condemned to a life of abject misery in a war of all against all. Looked at in this way, we can understand why Dostoevsky regarded "The Grand Inquisitor" as purely negative, an expression of Ivan's atheistic worldview. Its charge against Christianity is that, by formulating impossible ideals, Christianity has only increased our suffering on earth.

Ivan's account of the three temptations of Christ (from Matthew 4:1–11) reinforces the idea of this fundamental tension within Christianity. In the first temptation, when the devil calls on Jesus to turn stones into bread, Jesus replies, "Man does not live by bread alone." The Grand Inquisitor interprets this as a rejection of worldly comforts and a demand for absolute austerity and self-discipline. In the second temptation, Jesus is told to throw himself down from the top of the temple to prove that he will be miraculously saved. The Inquisitor interprets this as a rejection of miracle and mystery in this world. In the third temptation, Jesus is offered the world if he will worship Satan, and this the Inquisitor interprets as a demand for the total separation of church and state.

In each of these temptations the opposition is set up between the Protestant position (attributed to Christ) and the Roman Catholic position (the stance of the Inquisitor) as Ivan interprets these. But it is obvious that these issues extend well beyond a rather quirky interpretation of the two main branches of Western Christianity. For, as Ivan says, "all the unsolved contradictions of human nature" are embodied in these oppositions: those between Utilitarian and Kantian ethical theories, between welfare liberalism and free enterprise conservatism, and between Marxist-Leninist collectivism and Western rights-based individualism. The problem of reconciling the ideal of the greatest good of the greatest number with the ideal of individual responsibility and dignity seems as pressing today as it did a century ago.

Ivan's story presents a harsh indictment of Christianity. As we might expect, Alyosha is unable to see through what Ivan is up to in his story. He mimics Christ's kiss, not realizing how effete that makes Christ look, and he is deluded into thinking the legend is in fact a vindication of Christ. But on one point his hunch is right. He correctly sees that Ivan has laid out only the tenets of the *Western* forms of Christianity: "That's not the idea of the Orthodox Church," he exclaims, "That's Rome." In "The Russian Monk," Dostoevsky will try to respond to Ivan's dilemma by working out an alternative understanding of the significance of Christianity—that of the Eastern Orthodox Church.

Dostoevsky holds that, from within his rationalistic Enlightenment worldview, Ivan's challenge to Christianity is unanswerable. His approach to dealing with Ivan's critique, then, is not to try to present rational arguments against it, but to show that the existential stance from which Ivan's critique is presented is untenable. As we have seen, secular reformers like the Grand Inquisitor are motivated not so much by love of humanity as by overweening *pride*. Behind the Grand Inquisitor's show of brotherly love we see his true motivation: a desire for power. "We shall show them that they are weak, that they are only pitiful children," he says, describing how the "elect" will help the people. "They will become timid and will look to us and huddle close to us in fear, as chicks to the hen, . . . and they will adore us as their saviors who have taken on themselves their sins before God." What is really driving these self-anointed saviors of humanity, then, is something even Alyosha can see: "It's simple lust for power, for filthy earthly gain, for domination—something like a universal serfdom with them as masters—that's all they stand for."

The kind of egoism and grandiosity that motivates secular reformers is captured by the Russian word *samost'*. In *samost'*, a person "sets himself up as an individual, proprietor of his own nature, which he pits against the natures of others."[21] The outcome is a war of all

---

21. Vladimir Lossky, *The Mystical Theology of the Eastern Church* (Crestwood, N.Y.: St. Vladimir's Seminary Press, 1976), p. 122.

against all, with each person bent on "looking out for number one" and so inevitably caught in a power struggle with others. Dostoevsky thinks that this modern tendency toward self-aggrandizement and self-reliance is a result of Western ideas filtering down into Russia. The "mysterious visitor" in "The Russian Monk" describes modern individualism as a form of sickness spreading throughout the world.

> For everyone strives to keep his individuality as apart as possible, wishes to secure the greatest possible fullness of life for himself; but meantime all his efforts result not in attaining fullness of life but in self-destruction, for instead of self-realization, he ends by arriving at complete solitude. All mankind in our age have split up into units; they all keep apart, each in his own groove; each one holding himself aloof, hides himself and hides what he has from the rest, and he ends up by being repelled from others and re-pelling them.

The struggle for self-affirmation with its endless jockeying for posi-tion is a product of laceration, and it only produces isolation and contention. Ruled by the willful desire to be a self-reliant, masterful self, one ends up being cut off from the sources of true happiness and fulfillment.

Dostoevsky's diagnosis of egoism and individualism draws on a central tenet of the Christian tradition: the belief that God has given us a proper place in the scheme of things, so that any attempt to be more than what we are only makes us less than human. This is the view of St. Augustine when he says that God has placed us midway between the angels and the beasts, and that any attempt to deny our creatureliness, to be like the angels, will leave us no better than the beasts. "Beginning from a perverse desire to be as God is, beneath no one," he says, "one is hurled in punishment from one's proper middle place to the lowest place where the beasts delight to be." Starting from a desire to be like God, such a life "arrives in the end at likeness to the beasts."[22]

What is the cure for pride and egoism? We can understand Dostoev-sky's answer only if we try to understand one of the deepest strands of Russian spirituality—the immense importance accorded to "kenoti-cism" as a way of life. *Kenosis* refers to Christ's act of self-emptying—his submission to the most extreme humiliation and suffering in order to do the will of the Father. In Russian belief, this self-abasement and

22. *De Trinitate* (12.11.16).

self-abnegation has set a model for all humanity. To live the kenotic way of life is to follow the example of Christ, acceping suffering in meekness and humility. Dostoevsky believed that the Russian peasants still embody a capacity for such self-sacrifice and selfless love, though this ideal of the *Imitatio Christi* has been clouded over by Western ideas introduced by the upper classes. Some of the most touching scenes in the book are those in which simple peasant women, who have suffered crushing losses, find solace from Father Zossima's exhortations to accept their suffering in Christlike peace of mind. The image of Christ shows us that we should embrace our concrete being on earth, with all its suffering and joys, without trying to be more than what we are. In Dostoevsky's words, "Christ walked on earth to show mankind that even in its earthly nature the human spirit can manifest itself in heavenly radiance, in the flesh, and not merely in dream or ideal."[23]

The only way to achieve release from egoistic individualism, then, is through an act of surrender. We must be freed from our own willfulness in order to become part of God's will radiating into the world. The importance of release or surrender is conveyed in the words from the Gospel of John (12:24) that Dostoevsky takes as the epigraph of *The Brothers Karamazov*: "Verily, verily I say unto you, except a corn of wheat fall into the ground and dies, it abideth alone; but if it die, it bringeth forth much fruit."

The image of dying to oneself in order to be reborn into God's grace is fundamental to the entire Christian tradition. It lies at the heart of St. Paul's words, "Be ye like unto a newborn child." And it is the basis for the simple, heartfelt expression of humility in the well-known prayer of St. Francis: "Lord, make me a channel of thy peace, that where there is hatred I may bring love, that where there is wrong I may bring forgiveness, that where there is strife I may bring harmony. . . ." In the prayer we find the paradox that victory is achieved through surrender: "For it is by self-forgetting that one finds. It is by forgiving that one is forgiven." And its concluding words express the conviction that it is only through self-loss—through total release from the ego—that one finds true fulfillment: "It is by dying that one awakens to eternal life." Only by emptying out the ego, dying to one's own self, can one become an instrument of God's will. In the light of

23. Notes for *The Possessed*, quoted by V. V. Zenkovsky, "Dostoevsky's Religious and Philosophical Views," in Wellek, *Dostoevsky: A Collection of Critical Essays*, p. 137.

this kenotic experience we can see how the secular reformers have poisoned the springs of Russian faith and have cut themselves off from the sources of healing that alone can bring about happiness for the people of Russia.

The stark dichotomies Ivan creates in his Grand Inquisitor story reflect his own lacerated stance toward life. Ivan's dilemma is this. *Either* we follow the Protestant path and aim for human perfection in isolation and misery, *or* we strive for human happiness and peace in a vast totalitarian state where all freedom and dignity are abandoned. The first thing to note about this dilemma is that it can get off the ground only if we accept some basic assumptions about the human condition that are taken as self-evident and beyond discussion. Ivan assumes that at the deepest level humans are isolated individuals with no real bonds to one another, living in an essentially meaningless, value-neutral mechanistic universe, motivated solely by self-interest. If there is a God on such a view, He could be nothing but an occult entity located *outside* the world—a despot sitting on high, with no real connection to life on this earth.

Given these assumptions, there seem to be only two possibilities. Either we follow the path attributed to Christ and learn to live with our isolation, seeking fulfillment for ourselves while accepting the fact that the vast majority of our fellow humans will be condemned to a life of misery. Or we follow the Grand Inquisitor and dedicate ourselves to bringing happiness and security to the masses of humans. But since people will not accept a system of government unless they feel it has some higher sanction, this second option can be realized only by deluding people into thinking that there is a dimension of mystery or spiritual significance to life. Hence, the Grand Inquisitor concludes that in order to control the weak and unruly masses it will be necessary to superimpose the trappings of religion onto life—to create an aura of "miracle, mystery, and authority"—to give people a sense of shared purpose and community of worship. What is needed is something like the sorts of mystification that backed up the crypto-religion of the Soviet Union: miraculous Five Year Plans, Proletarian Heroes, personality cults, faith in Party infallibility, messianic fervor in the quest for world communism, and so on.

Ivan's claim is that we must choose between these two options—

either freedom in misery or happiness as slaves—though both options are equally intolerable. A little reflection should show, however, that the dilemma is inescapable only if we accept the basic assumptions about the human condition Ivan has picked up from the West.

Dostoevsky's way of dealing with the Grand Inquisitor story is to challenge Ivan's basic assumptions. He tries to show, first of all, that the Western conceptions of both freedom and happiness presupposed in the dilemma are incoherent. With respect to the notion of freedom, Dostoevsky suggests that the Western understanding of freedom as the absence of constraint—as the ability to do anything you want—turns out to be nothing but slavery to one's every passing whim and caprice: "Interpreting freedom as the multiplication and rapid satisfaction of desires, men distort their own nature, for many senseless and foolish desires . . . are fostered in them." True freedom, in contrast, is achieved when we can free ourselves from transient, self-centered cravings and commit ourselves to accomplishing something of value in the world: "I cut off my superfluous and unnecessary desires," Zossima says. "I subdue my proud and wanton will and chastise it with obedience, and with God's help I attain freedom of spirit and with it spiritual joy." Far from being the opposite of happiness, such freedom is a necessary condition for achieving true happiness.

In a similar way Dostoevsky tries to show that the concept of happiness presupposed in the dilemma is incoherent. The West interprets happiness as the pleasurable feeling we get from having our desires filled, and it imagines true happiness to be the instant gratification of every desire. Yet, as the Grand Inquisitor sees, this sort of "pleasure principle" threatens to lead to conflict among individuals who are in competition for limited resources, and for this reason he concludes that happiness will be possible only in a totalitarian state. What Dostoevsky points out, in contrast, is that a life given over to the pursuit of good feelings is self-defeating. For every time we succeed in getting what we want, we have a feeling of emptiness, and that in turn creates a new craving for pleasure. The result is an endless cycle of pleasures followed by feelings of emptiness followed by frenzied attempts to feel pleasure. The outcome, quite obviously, is a feeling of futility and despair. In opposition to this conception of happiness as pleasure, Dostoevsky suggests that genuine happiness is found in the inner peace that comes from accepting life, together with all its joys and sufferings, on life's own terms. Zossima's "answer to Job," such as it is, is found not so much in a rational vindication of God's creation as in an evocation of the "softening, reconciling" power of the acceptance of suffering and grief: "It's the great mystery of human life that old grief passes gradually into quiet tender joy." It is by coming to understand life as suffused with such simple mysteries that we find true happiness and freedom.

Ivan's dilemma gains its force from the assumption that humans are fundamentally isolated individuals, and that any community must be an artificial construct superimposed over them by an external force. But Dostoevsky sees that there are indigenous forms of life within Russia that provide an alternative to this Western atomistic and objectified understanding of human existence. The age-old institution of the *mir* or village commune embodies a way of life in which people are initially and at the deepest level participants in a shared spiritual community, rooted in a horizon of values and meanings that define their understanding of what life is all about. What is "given" at such a level of experience is not the individual's lonely quest for self-fulfillment, but an experience of the harmony of "togetherness" or "belongingness" expressed in the Russian word *sobornost'*. From the standpoint of this primordial sense of the connectedness of life, the Western image of isolated individuals motivated solely by self-interest looks like a deformation of human nature rather than the bedrock "truth" about who we are.

Zossima's emphasis on the mystery running through everyday life stands in stark contrast to the sharp separation of sacred and profane in the West. For the Eastern Church, to pray that it will be "on earth as it is in heaven" implies that the sacred is not something promised for an "other" world, but is something that surrounds us here and now, permeating all of life, even though our pride keeps us from seeing it. Our aim in life, then, is not to get into an other world, but to work toward the deification of the world in which we find ourselves. In fact, since there is no personal salvation in the Eastern faith, but only salvation for creation as a whole, our only hope for salvation lies in self-forgetfulness and active love in the world. Thus, the doctrine of *sobornost'* points to the holistic vision of "salvation as a process of becoming divine, not only for men but for the whole created world."[24]

From this perspective, the divine is experienced as permeating all creation, filling everything with a spiritual significance. The only way

24. Donald Lowrie, quoted in Sandoz, *Political Apocalypse*, p. 147.

to see the sanctity of all creation, however, is to live a life of active love, the selfless love referred to by the Greek word *agape.* As Zossima says, "If you love everything, you will perceive the divine mystery in things. Once you perceive it, you will begin to comprehend it better every day. And you will come at last to love the whole world with an all-embracing love." We can now see that, to the extent Ivan's lacerated stance cuts him off from participating in life, he is incapable of the kind of love that would enable him to comprehend the mystery in all things.

Zossima's cosmic religious experience expresses the sense central to the Eastern Church that all nature embodies a sacred dimension, a sanctity which becomes apparent to us only in *agape.* Consider the words of St. Isaac the Syrian (whose writings are mentioned in *The Brothers Karamazov*):

> What is a charitable heart? It is a heart which is burning with charity for the whole creation, for people, for the birds, for the beasts, for the demons—for all creatures. He who has such a heart cannot see or call to mind a creature without his eyes becoming filled with tears by reason of the immense compassion which seizes his heart. . . . This is why such a person never ceases to pray also for the animals.[25]

This cosmic religious sense emerges in the rapturous visions of Zossima's dying brother, and its life-transforming power reappears years later when it saves Zossima from a cruel and brutal act. Refusing to fire his pistol in a pointless duel, he cries out,

> Gentlemen, . . . look around you at the gifts of God, the clear sky, the pure air, the tender grass, the birds; nature is beautiful and sinless, and we, only we, are sinful and foolish, and we don't understand that life is heaven, for we only have to understand that and it will at once be fulfilled in all its beauty.

In this mystical vision of the cosmos as a sanctified totality we can find an answer to Ivan's stance in "Rebellion." Recall that Ivan's conclusion there was that, given the suffering in the world, there is no way anyone can go on living without, in effect, condoning the suffering and so being partly guilty for what goes on. The only way to avoid having dirty hands, then, is to commit suicide. What Zossima's evoca-

25. Quoted in Lossky, *The Mystical Theology of the Eastern Church,* p. 111.

tion of the web of connectedness in the cosmos leads us to see, however, is that we all are indeed accomplices in the world, and so we *are* responsible and guilty for what occurs. But this recognition of responsibility points not to suicide, but to taking *action* in the world. Contrary to what Ivan thinks, we *must* be our brothers' keepers. Ivan's feeling that life is unjustified results from his lacerated stance which puts him in the position of a judge standing outside the world evaluating it. But it is precisely because that stance is motivated by pride and cuts him off from the world that it makes it impossible for him to see what can be done to improve the human condition. In fact, as we have seen, it tends to breed a second-order evil that intensifies the suffering that already exists.

In Dostoevsky's view, the only way to deal with the problem of suffering is to embrace our own responsibility for what happens in the world and to own up to it by *acting* to change things. This is the significance of Zossima's startling claim:

> There is only one means of salvation, then: take yourself and make yourself responsible for all men's sins, . . . for as soon as you sincerely make yourself responsible for everything and for all men, you will see at once that it really is so, and that you are to blame for everyone and for all things.

The deep sense of the connectedness and oneness of all things within the cosmos provides an antidote to Ivan's atomistic and objectified worldview. Ivan is right to say that we are all accomplices in a scheme of things where suffering exists. But recognizing this is only the first step. For, insofar as we are all already involved, we also have an obligation to try to improve things. The answer to the problem of suffering is reached not through a theoretical insight, then, but through *action* that flows from this vision of connectedness and spiritual significance.

Charles B. Guignon

THE GRAND
INQUISITOR

BOOK V

PRO AND CONTRA

CHAPTER 3

The Brothers Make Friends

Ivan was not, however, in a separate room, but only in a place shut off by a screen, so that it was unseen by other people in the room. It was the first room from the entrance, with a buffet along the wall. Waiters were continually darting to and fro in it. . . .

Ivan rang for the waiter and ordered soup, jam, and tea.

"I remember everything, Alyosha. I remember you till you were eleven; I was nearly fifteen. There's such a difference between fifteen and eleven that brothers are never companions at those ages. I don't know whether I was fond of you even. When I went away to Moscow, for the first few years I never thought of you at all. Then, when you came to Moscow yourself, we only met once somewhere, I believe. And now I've been here more than three months, and so far we have scarcely said a word to each other. Tomorrow I am going away, and I was just thinking as I sat here how I could see you to say good-bye, and just then you passed."

"Were you very anxious to see me then?"

"Very. I want to get to know you once and for all, and I want you to know me. And then to say good-bye. I believe it's always best to get to know people just before leaving them. I've noticed how you've been looking at me these three months. There has been a continual look of expectation in your eyes, and I can't endure that. That's why I've kept away from you. But in the end I have learned to respect you. The little man stands firm, I thought. Though I am laughing, I am serious. You do stand firm, don't you? I like people who are firm like that, whatever it is they stand by, even if they are such little fellows as you. Your expectant eyes ceased to annoy me; I grew fond of them in the end, those expectant eyes. You seem to love me for some reason, Alyosha?"

"I do love you, Ivan. Dmitri says of you—Ivan is a tomb! I say of you, Ivan is a riddle. You are a riddle to me even now. But I understand something in you, and I did not understand it till this morning."

"What's that?" laughed Ivan.

"You won't be angry?" Alyosha laughed too.

"Well?"

"That you are just as young as other young men of twenty-three, that you are just a young and fresh and nice boy, green in fact! Now, have I insulted you dreadfully?"

"On the contrary, I am struck by a coincidence," cried Ivan, warmly and good-humouredly. "Would you believe it that ever since [this morning], I have thought of nothing else but my youthful greenness, and just as though you guessed that, you begin about it. Do you know, I've been sitting here thinking to myself that if I didn't believe in life, if I lost faith in the woman I love, lost faith in the order of things, were convinced in fact that everything is a disorderly, damnable, and perhaps devil-ridden chaos, if I were struck by every horror of man's disillusionment—still I should want to live and, having once tasted of the cup, I would not turn away from it till I had drained it! At thirty, though, I shall be sure to leave the cup, even if I've not emptied it, and turn away—where I don't know. But until I am thirty, I know that my youth will triumph over everything—every disillusionment, every disgust with life. I've asked myself many times whether there is in the world any despair that would overcome this frantic and perhaps unseemly thirst for life in me, and I've come to the conclusion that there isn't, that is, until I am thirty, and then I shall lose it of myself, I fancy. Some drivelling consumptive moralists—and poets especially—often call that thirst for life base. It's a feature of the Karamazovs, it's true, that thirst for life regardless of everything; you have it no doubt too, but why is it base? The centripetal force on our planet is still fearfully strong, Alyosha. I have a longing for life, and I go on living in spite of logic. Though I may not believe in the order of the universe, yet I love the sticky little leaves as they open in spring. I love the blue sky, I love some people, whom one loves, you know, sometimes without knowing why. I love some great deeds done by men, though I've long ceased perhaps to have faith in them, yet from old habit one's heart prizes them. . . . I want to travel in Europe, Alyosha; I shall set off from here. I know that I am only going to a graveyard, but it's a most precious graveyard, that's what it is! Precious are the dead that lie there; every stone over them speaks of such burning life in the past, of such passionate faith in their work, their truth, their struggle, and their science, that I know I shall fall on the ground and kiss those stones and weep over them, though I'm convinced in my heart that it's long been nothing but a graveyard. And I shall not weep from despair, but simply because I shall be happy in my tears. I shall steep my soul in my emotion. I love the sticky leaves in spring, the blue sky—that's all it is. It's not a matter of intellect or logic; it's loving with one's inside, with one's stomach. One loves the first strength of one's youth. Do you understanding anything of my tirade, Alyosha?" Ivan laughed suddenly.

"I understand too well, Ivan. One longs to love with one's inside, with one's stomach. You said that so well, and I am awfully glad that you have such a longing for life," cried Alyosha. "I think everyone should love life above everything in the world."

"Love life more than the meaning of it?"

"Certainly, love it regardless of logic as you say; it must be regardless of logic, and it's only then one will understand the meaning of it. I have thought so a long time. Half your work is done, Ivan. You love life; now you've only to try to do the second half and you are saved."

"You are trying to save me, but perhaps I am not lost! And what does your second half mean?"

"Why, one has to raise up your dead, who perhaps have not died after all. . . . "

* * * * *

"It's different for other people, but we in our green youth have to settle the eternal questions first of all," [said Ivan]. "That's what we care about. Young Russia is talking about nothing but the eternal questions now. Just when the old folks are all taken up with practical questions. Why have you been looking at me in expectation for the last three months? To ask me, 'what do you believe, or don't you believe at all?' That's what your eyes have been saying these last three months, haven't they?"

"Perhaps so," smiled Alyosha. "You are not laughing at me now, are you, Ivan?"

"Me laughing? I don't want to wound my little brother, who has been watching me with such expectation for three months. Alyosha, look straight at me! Of course, I am just such a little boy as you are, only not a novice. And what have Russian boys been doing up till now, some of them, I mean? In this stinking tavern, for instance, they meet and sit down in a corner. They've never met in their lives before and, when they go out of the tavern, they won't meet again for forty years. And what do they talk about in that momentary halt in the tavern? Of the eternal questions, of the existence of God, and immortality. And those who do not believe in God talk of socialism or anarchism, of the transformation of all humanity on a new pattern, so that it all comes to the same; they're the same questions turned inside out. And masses, masses of the most original Russian boys do nothing but talk of the eternal questions! Isn't it so?"

"Yes, for real Russians, the questions of God's existence and of immortality, or, as you say, the same questions turned inside out, come first and foremost. Of course, and so they should," said Alyosha, still watching his brother with the same gentle and inquiring smile.

"Well, Alyosha, it's sometimes very unwise to be a Russian at all, but anything stupider than the way Russian boys spend their time one can hardly imagine. But there's one Russian boy called Alyosha I am awfully fond of."

"How nicely you put that in!" Alyosha laughed suddenly.

"Well, tell me where to begin, give your orders. The existence of God, eh?"

"Begin where you like. You declared yesterday at father's that there is no God." Alyosha looked searchingly at his brother.

"I said that yesterday at dinner on purpose to tease you, and I saw your eyes glow. But now I've no objection to discussing it with you, and I say so very seriously. I want to be friends with you, Alyosha, for I have no friends and want to try it. Well, only fancy, perhaps I too accept God," laughed Ivan, "that's a surprise for you, isn't it?"

"Yes, of course, if you are not joking now."

"Joking? I was told at the elder's yesterday that I was joking. You know, dear boy, there was an old sinner in the eighteenth century who declared that, if there were no God, he would have to be invented. *S'il n'existait pas Dieu, il faudrait l'inventer.** And man has actually invented God. And what's strange, what would be marvellous, is not that God should really exist; the marvel is that such an idea, the idea of the necessity of God, could enter the head of such a savage, vicious beast as man. So holy it is, so touching, so wise, and so great a credit it does to man. As for me, I've long resolved not to think about whether man

---

*"If God did not exist, it would be necessary to invent him."

created God or God man. And I won't go through all the axioms laid down by Russian boys on that subject, all derived from European hypotheses; for what's a hypothesis there, is an axiom with the Russian boy, and not only with the boys but with their teachers, too, for our Russian professors are often just the same boys themselves. And so I omit all the hypotheses. For what are we aiming at now? I am trying to explain as quickly as possible my essential nature, that is, what manner of man I am, what I believe in, and what I hope for; that's it, isn't it? And therefore I tell you that I accept God simply. But you must note this: if God exists and if He really did create the world, then, as we all know, He created it according to the geometry of Euclid and the human mind with the conception of only three dimensions in space. Yet there have been and still are geometricians and philosophers, and even some of the most distinguished, who doubt whether the whole universe, or to speak more widely the whole of being, was only created in Euclid's geometry; they even dare to dream that two parallel lines, which according to Euclid can never meet on earth, may meet somewhere in infinity. I have come to the conclusion that, since I can't understand even that, I can't expect to understand about God. I acknowledge humbly that I have no faculty for settling such questions; I have a Euclidian earthly mind, and how could I solve problems that are not of this world? And I advise you never to think about it either, my dear Alyosha, especially about God, whether He exists or not. All such questions are utterly inappropriate for a mind created with an idea of only three dimensions. And so I accept God and am glad to, and what's more I accept His wisdom, His purpose—which are utterly beyond our ken; I believe in the underlying order and the meaning of life; I believe in the eternal harmony in which they say we shall one day be blended. I believe in the Word to Which the universe is striving, and Which Itself was "with God," and Which Itself is God, and so on, and so on, to infinity. There are all sorts of phrases for it. I seem to be on the right path, don't I? Yet, would you believe it, in the final result I don't accept this world of God's, and, although I know it exists, I don't accept it at all. It's not that I don't accept God, you must understand; it's the world created by Him I don't and cannot accept. Let me make it plain. I believe like a child that suffering will be healed and made up for; that all the humiliating absurdity of human contradictions will vanish like a pitiful mirage, like the despicable fabrication of the impotent and infinitely small Euclidian mind of man; that in the world's finale, at the moment of eternal harmony,

something so precious will come to pass that it will suffice for all
hearts, for the comforting of all resentments, for the atonement of all
the crimes of humanity, of all the blood they've shed; that it will make
it not only possible to forgive but to justify all that has happened with
men—but though all that may come to pass, I don't accept it. I won't
accept it. Even if parallel lines do meet and I see it myself, I shall see
it and say that they've met, but still I won't accept it. That's what's at
the root of me, Alyosha; that's my creed. I am in earnest in what I
say. I began our talk as stupidly as I could on purpose, but I've led up
to my confession, for that's all you want. You didn't want to hear about
God, but only to know what the brother you love lives by. And so I've
told you."

Ivan concluded his long tirade with marked and unexpected feeling.

"And why did you begin 'as stupidly as you could'?" asked Alyosha,
looking thoughtfully at him.

"To begin with, for the sake of being Russian. Russian conversations on such subjects are always carried on inconceivably stupidly.
And, secondly, the stupider one is, the closer one is to reality. The
stupider one is, the clearer one is. Stupidity is brief and artless, while
intelligence wriggles and hides itself. Intelligence is a knave, but stupidity is honest and straightforward. I've led the conversation to my
despair, and the more stupidly I have presented it, the better for me."

"You will explain why you don't accept the world?" said Alyosha.

"To be sure I will. It's not a secret; that's what I've been leading up
to. Dear little brother, I don't want to corrupt you or to turn you from
your stronghold; perhaps I want to be healed by you." Ivan smiled
suddenly quite like a little gentle child. Alyosha had never seen such a
smile on his face before.

BOOK V

CHAPTER 4

Rebellion

"I must make you one confession," Ivan began. "I could never understand how one can love one's neighbors. It's just one's neighbors, to my mind, that one can't love, though one might love those at a distance. I once read somewhere of John the Merciful, a saint, that when a hungry, frozen beggar came to him, he took him into his bed, held him in his arms, and began breathing into his mouth, which was putrid and loathsome from some awful disease. I am convinced that he did that from 'self-laceration,' from the self-laceration of falsity, for the sake of the charity imposed by duty, as a penance laid on him. For anyone to love a man, he must be hidden, for as soon as he shows his face, love is gone."

"Father Zossima has talked of that more than once," observed Alyosha. "He, too, said that the face of a man often hinders many people not practiced in love, from loving him. But still there's a great deal of love in mankind, an almost Christlike love. I know that myself, Ivan."

"Well, I know nothing of it so far, and can't understand it, and the innumerable mass of mankind are with me there. The question is whether that's due to men's bad qualities or whether it's inherent in their nature. To my thinking, Christlike love for men is a miracle impossible on earth. He was God. But we are not gods. Suppose I, for instance, suffer intensely. Another can never know how much I suffer, because he is another and not I. And what's more, a man is rarely ready to admit another's suffering (as though it were a distinction). Why won't he admit it, do you think? Because I smell unpleasant; because I have a stupid face; because I once trod on his foot. Besides, there is suffering and suffering. Degrading, humiliating suffering, such as humbles me—hunger, for instance—my benefactor will perhaps allow me; but when you come to higher suffering—for an idea, for instance—he will very rarely admit that, perhaps because my face strikes him as not at all what he fancies a man should have who suffers for an idea. And so he deprives me instantly of his favor, and not at all from badness of heart. Beggars, especially genteel beggars, ought never to show themselves, but to ask for charity through the newspapers. One can love one's neighbors in the abstract, or even at a distance, but at close quarters it's almost impossible. If it were as on the stage, in the ballet, where if beggars come in, they wear silken rags and tattered lace, and beg for alms dancing gracefully, then one might like looking at them. But even then we should not love them. But enough of that. I simply wanted to show you my point of view. I meant to speak of the suffering of mankind generally, but we had better confine ourselves to the sufferings of the children. That reduces the scope of my argument to a tenth of what it would be. Still we'd better keep to the children, though it does weaken my case. But, in the first place, children can be loved even at close quarters, even when they are dirty, even when they are ugly (I suspect, though, that children never are ugly). The second reason why I won't speak of grownup people is that, besides being disgusting and unworthy of love, they have a compensation—they've eaten the apple and know good and evil, and they have become 'like god.' They go on eating it still. But the children haven't eaten anything, and are so far innocent. Are you fond of children, Alyosha? I know you are, and you will understand why I prefer to speak of them. If they too suffer horribly on earth, they must suffer for their fathers' sins; they must be punished for their fathers, who have eaten the apple; but that reasoning is of the other world and is incomprehensible for the heart of man here on earth. The innocent must not suffer for another's sins, and especially such innocents! You may be surprised at me, Alyosha, but I am awfully fond of children too. And observe: cruel people—the violent, the rapacious, the Karamazovs—are sometimes very fond of children. Children while they are quite little—up to seven, for instance—are so remote from grownup people, they are different creatures, as it were, of a different species. I knew a criminal in prison who had, in the course of his career as a burglar, murdered whole families, including several children. But when he was in prison, he had a strange affection for them. He spent all his time at his window, watching the children playing in the prison yard. He trained one little boy to come up to his window and made great friends with him. . . . You don't know why I am telling you all this, Alyosha? My head aches and I am sad."

"You speak with a strange air," observed Alyosha uneasily, "as though you were not quite yourself."

"By the way, a Bulgarian I met lately in Moscow," Ivan went on, seeming not to hear his brother's words, "told me about the crimes committed by Turks and Circassians in all parts of Bulgaria through fear of a general rising of the Slavs. They burn villages, murder, outrage women and children; they nail their prisoners by the ears to the fences, leave them so till morning, and in the morning they hang them—all sorts of things you can't imagine. People talk sometimes of bestial cruelty, but that's a great injustice and insult to the beasts; a beast can never be so cruel as a man, so artistically cruel. The tiger only tears and gnaws, that's all he can do. He would never think of nailing people by the ears, even if he were able to do it. These Turks took a pleasure in torturing children, too; cutting the unborn child from the mother's womb, and tossing babies up in the air, and catching them on the points of their bayonets before their mother's eyes. Doing it before the mother's eyes was what gave zest to the amusement. Here is another scene that I thought very interesting. Imagine a trembling mother with her baby in her arms, a circle of invading Turks around her. They've planned a diversion; they pet the baby, laugh to make it laugh. They succeed; the baby laughs. At that moment, a Turk points a pistol four inches from the baby's face. The baby laughs with glee, holds out its little hands to the pistol, and he pulls the trigger in the baby's face and blows out its brains. Artistic, wasn't it? By the way, Turks are particularly fond of sweet things, they say."

"Brother, what are you driving at?" asked Alyosha.

"I think if the devil doesn't exist, but man has created him, he has created him in his own image and likeness."

"Just as he did God, then?" observed Alyosha.

"'It's wonderful how you can turn words,' as Polonius says in *Hamlet*," laughed Ivan. "You turn my words against me. Well, I am glad. Yours must be a fine God, if man created Him in His image and likeness. You asked just now what I was driving at. You see, I am fond of collecting certain facts, and, would you believe it, I even copy anecdotes of a certain sort from newspapers and books, and I've already got a fine collection. The Turks, of course, have gone into it, but they are foreigners. I have specimens from home that are even better than the Turks. You know we prefer beating—rods and scourges—that's our national institution. Nailing ears is unthinkable for us, for

we are, after all, Europeans. But the rod and the scourge we have
always with us, and they cannot be taken from us. Abroad now they
scarcely do any beating. Manners are more humane, or laws have been
passed so that they don't dare to flog men now. But they make up for it
in another way just as national as ours. And so national that it would
be practically impossible among us, though I believe we are being
inoculated with it, since the religious movement began in our aristoc-
racy. I have a charming pamphlet, translated from the French, describing how, quite recently, five years ago, a murderer, Richard, was
executed—a young man, I believe, of twenty-three, who repented and
was converted to the Christian faith at the very scaffold. This Richard
was an illegitimate child who was given as a child of six by his parents
to some shepherds on the Swiss mountains. They brought him up to
work for them. He grew up like a little wild beast among them. The
shepherds taught him nothing, and scarcely fed or clothed him, but
sent him out at seven to herd the flock in the cold and wet, and no one
hesitated or scrupled to treat him so. Quite the contrary; they thought
they had every right, for Richard had been given to them as a chattel,
and they did not even see the necessity of feeding him. Richard
himself describes how in those years, like the Prodigal Son in the
Gospel, he longed to eat of the mash given to the pigs, which were
fattened for sale. But they wouldn't even give him that, and beat him
when he stole from the pigs. And that was how he spent all his
childhood and his youth, till he grew up and was strong enough to go
away and be a thief. The savage began to earn his living as a day
laborer in Geneva. He drank what he earned, he lived like a brute,
and finished by killing and robbing an old man. He was caught, tried,
and condemned to death. They are not sentimentalists there. And in
prison he was immediately surrounded by pastors, members of Christian brotherhoods, philanthropic ladies, and the like. They taught him
to read and write in prison, and expounded the Gospel to him. They
exhorted him, worked upon him, drummed at him incessantly, till at
last he solemnly confessed his crime. He was converted. He wrote to
the court himself that he was a monster, but that in the end God had
vouchsafed him light and shown grace. All Geneva was in excitement
about him—all philanthropic and religious Geneva. All the aristocratic and wellbred society of the town rushed to the prison, kissed
Richard and embraced him; 'You are our brother; you have found
grace.' And Richard does nothing but weep with emotion. "Yes, I've
found grace! All my youth and childhood I was glad of pigs' food, but

now even I have found grace. I am dying in the Lord.' 'Yes, Richard, die in the Lord; you have shed blood and must die. Though it's not your fault that you knew not the Lord, when you coveted the pigs' food and were beaten for stealing it (which was very wrong of you, for stealing is forbidden). But you've shed blood and you must die.' And on the last day, Richard, perfectly limp, did nothing but cry and repeat every minute, 'This is my happiest day. I am going to the Lord.' 'Yes,' cry the pastors and the judges and philanthropic ladies. 'This is the happiest day of your life, for you are going to the Lord!' They all walk or drive to the scaffold in procession behind the prison van. At the scaffold they call to Richard, 'Die, brother, die in the Lord, for even thou hast found grace!' And so, covered with his brothers' kisses, Richard is dragged on to the scaffold, and led to the guillotine. And they chopped off his head in brotherly fashion, because he had found grace. Yes, that's characteristic. That pamphlet is translated into Russian by some Russian philanthropists of aristocratic rank and evangelical aspirations, and has been distributed gratis for the enlightenment of the people. The case of Richard is interesting because it's national. Though to us it's absurd to cut off a man's head because he has become our brother and has found grace, yet we have our own specialty, which is all but worse. Our historical pastime is the direct satisfaction of inflicting pain. There are lines in Nekrassov describing how a peasant lashes a horse on the eyes, 'on its meek eyes.' Everyone must have seen it; it's peculiarly Russian. He describes how a feeble little nag has foundered under too heavy a load and cannot move. The peasant beats it, beats it savagely, beats it at last not knowing what he is doing in the intoxication of cruelty, thrashes it mercilessly over and over again. 'However weak you are, you must pull, even if you die for it.' The nag strains. And then he begins lashing the poor defenceless creature on its weeping, on its 'meek eyes.' The frantic beast tugs and draws the load, trembling all over, gasping for breath, moving sideways, with a sort of unnatural spasmodic action—it's awful in Nekrassov. But that's only a horse, and God has given horses to be beaten. So the Tatars have taught us, and they left us the knout as a remembrance of it. But men, too, can be beaten. A well-educated, cultured gentleman and his wife beat their own child with a birch rod, a girl of seven. I have an exact account of it. The papa was glad that the birch was covered with twigs. 'It stings more,' said he, and so he began stinging his daughter. I know for a fact there are people who at every blow are worked up to sensuality, to literal sensuality, which increases progressively at every blow they inflict. They beat for a minute, for five minutes, for ten minutes, more often and more savagely. The child screams. At last the child cannot scream; it gasps, 'Daddy! daddy!' By some diabolical, unseemly chance the case was brought into court. A counsel is engaged. The Russian people have long called a barrister 'a conscience for hire.' The counsel protests in his client's defence. 'It's such a simple thing,' he says, 'an everyday domestic event. A father corrects his child. To our shame be it said, it is brought into court.' The jury, convinced by him, gives a favorable verdict. The public roars with delight that the torturer is acquitted. Ah, pity I wasn't there! I would have proposed to raise a subscription in his honor! . . . Charming pictures.

"But I've still better things about children. I've collected a great, great deal about Russian children, Alyosha. There was a little girl of five who was hated by her father and mother, 'most worthy and respectable people, of good education and breeding.' You see, I must repeat again, it is a peculiar characteristic of many people, this love of torturing children, and children only. To all other types of humanity these torturers behave mildly and benevolently, like cultivated and humane Europeans; but they are very fond of tormenting children, even fond of children themselves in that sense. It's just their defence-lessness that tempts the tormentor, just the angelic confidence of the child who has no refuge and no appeal, that sets his vile blood on fire. In every man, of course, a demon lies hidden—the demon of rage, the demon of lustful heat at the screams of the tortured victim, the demon of lawlessness let off the chain, the demon of diseases that follow on vice, gout, kidney disease, and so on.

"This poor child of five was subjected to every possible torture by those cultivated parents. They beat her, thrashed her, kicked her for no reason till her body was one bruise. Then, they went to greater refinements of cruelty—shut her up all night in the cold and frost in a privy, and because she didn't ask to be taken up at night (as though a child of five sleeping its angelic, sound sleep could be trained to wake and ask), they smeared her face and filled her mouth with excrement, and it was her mother, her mother who did this. And that mother could sleep, hearing the poor child's groans! Can you understand why a little creature, who can't even understand what's done to her, should beat her little aching heart with her tiny fist in the dark and the cold, and weep her meek unresentful tears to dear, kind God to protect her? Do you understand that, friend and brother, you pious and humble novice? Do you understand why this infamy must be and is permitted? Without it, I am told, man could not have existed on earth, for he could not have known good and evil. Why should he know that diabolical good and evil when it costs so much? Why, the whole world of knowledge is not worth that child's prayer to 'dear, kind God'! I say nothing of the sufferings of grownup people; they have eaten the apple, damn them, and the devil take them all! But these little ones! I am making you suffer, Alyosha; you are not yourself. I'll leave off if you like."

"Never mind. I want to suffer too," muttered Alyosha.

"One picture, only one more, because it's so curious, so characteristic, and I have only just read it in some collection of Russian antiquities. I've forgotten the name. I must look it up. It was in the darkest days of serfdom at the beginning of the century, and long live the Liberator of the People! There was in those days a general of aristocratic connections, the owner of great estates, one of those men— somewhat exceptional, I believe, even then—who, retiring from the service into a life of leisure, are convinced that they've earned absolute power over the lives of their subjects. There were such men then. So our general, settled on his property of two thousand souls, lives in pomp, and domineers over his poor neighbors as though they were dependents and buffoons. He has kennels of hundreds of hounds and nearly a hundred dog boys—all mounted and in uniform. One day a serf boy, a little child of eight, threw a stone in play and hurt the paw of the general's favorite hound. 'Why is my favorite dog lame?' He is told that the boy threw a stone that hurt the dog's paw. 'So you did it.' The general looked the child up and down. 'Take him.' He was taken—taken from his mother and kept shut up all night. Early that morning the general comes out on horseback, with the hounds, his dependents, dog boys, and huntsmen, all mounted around him in full hunting parade. The servants are summoned for their edification, and in front of them all stands the mother of the child. The child is brought from the lockup. It's a gloomy, cold, foggy autumn day, a capital day for hunting. The general orders the child to be undressed; the child is stripped naked. He shivers, numb with terror, not daring to cry. . . . 'Make him run,' commands the general. 'Run! run!' shout the dog boys. The boy runs. . . . 'At him!' yells the general, and he sets the whole pack of hounds on the child. The hounds catch him, and tear him to pieces before his mother's eyes! . . . I believe the general was afterwards declared incapable of administering his estates. Well—what did he deserve? To be shot? To be shot for the satisfaction of our moral feelings? Speak, Alyosha!"

"To be shot," murmured Alyosha, lifting his eyes to Ivan with a pale, twisted smile.

"Bravo!" cried Ivan delighted. "If even you say so . . . You're a pretty monk! So there is a little devil sitting in your heart, Alyosha Karamazov!"

"What I said was absurd, but—"

"That's just the point, that 'but'!" cried Ivan. "Let me tell you, novice, that the absurd is only too necessary on earth. The world stands on absurdities, and perhaps nothing would have come to pass in it without them. We know what we know!"

"What do you know?"

"I understand nothing," Ivan went on, as though in a delirium. "I don't want to understand anything now. I want to stick to the fact. I made up my mind long ago not to understand. If I try to understand anything, I shall be false to the fact, and I have determined to stick to the fact."

"Why are you trying me?" Alyosha cried, with sudden distress. "Will you say what you mean at last?"

"Of course, I will; that's what I've been leading up to. You are dear to me. I don't want to let you go, and I won't give you up to your Zossima."

Ivan for a minute was silent; his face became all at once very sad.

"Listen! I took the case of children only to make my case clearer. Of the other tears of humanity with which the earth is soaked from its crust to its center, I will say nothing. I have narrowed my subject on purpose. I am a bug, and I recognize in all humility that I cannot understand why the world is arranged as it is. Men are themselves to blame, I suppose; they were given paradise, they wanted freedom, and stole fire from heaven, though they knew they would become unhappy, so there is no need to pity them. With my pitiful, earthly, Euclidian understanding, all I know is that there is suffering and that there are none guilty; that effect follows cause, simply and directly; that everything flows and finds it level—but that's only Euclidian nonsense, I know that, and I can't consent to live by it! What comfort is it to me that there are none guilty and that effect follows cause simply and directly, and that I know it—I must have justice, or I will destroy myself. And not justice in some remote infinite time and space, but here on earth, and that I could see myself. I have believed in it. I want to see it, and if I am dead by then, let me rise again, for if it all happens without me, it will be too unfair. Surely I haven't suffered, simply that I, my crimes and my sufferings, may manure the soil of the future harmony for somebody else. I want to see with my own eyes the hind lie down with the lion and the victim rise up and embrace his murderer. I want to be there when everyone suddenly understands what it has all been for. All the religions of the world are built on this longing, and I am a believer. But then there are the children, and what am I to do about them? That's a question I can't answer. For the hundredth time I repeat, there are numbers of questions, but I've only taken the children, because in their case what I mean is so unanswerably clear. Listen! If all must suffer to pay for the eternal harmony, what have children to do with it, tell me, please? It's beyond all comprehension why they should suffer, and why they should pay for the harmony. Why should they, too, furnish material to enrich the soil for the harmony of the future? I understand solidarity in sin among men. I understand solidarity in retribution, too; but there can be no such solidarity with children. And if it is really true that they must share responsibility for all their fathers' crimes, such a truth is not of this world and is beyond my comprehension. Some jester will say, perhaps, that the child would have grown up and have sinned, but you see he didn't grow up, he was torn to pieces by the dogs, at eight years old. Oh, Alyosha, I am not blaspheming! I understand, of course, what an upheaval of the universe it will be, when everything in heaven and earth blends in one hymn of praise and everything that lives and has lived cries aloud: 'Thou art just, O Lord, for Thy ways are revealed.' When the mother embraces the fiend who threw her child to the dogs, and all three cry aloud with tears, 'Thou are just, O Lord!' then, of course, the crown of knowledge will be reached and all will be made clear. But what pulls me up here is that I can't accept that harmony. And while I am on earth, I make haste to take my own measures. You see, Alyosha, perhaps it really may happen that if I live to that moment, or rise again to see it, I, too, perhaps, may cry aloud with the rest, looking at the mother embracing the child's torturer, 'Thou art just, O Lord!' But I don't want to cry aloud then. While there is still time, I hasten to protect myself, and so I renounce the higher harmony altogether. It's not worth the tears of that one tortured child who beat itself on the breast with its little fist and prayed in its stinking outhouse, with its unexpiated tears to 'dear, kind God'! It's not worth it, because those tears are unatoned for. They must be atoned for, or there can be no harmony. But how? How are you going to atone for them? Is it possible? By their being avenged? But what do I care for avenging them? What do I care for a hell for oppressors? What good can hell do, since those children have already been tortured? And what becomes of harmony, if there is hell? I want to forgive. I want to embrace. I don't want more suffering. And if the sufferings of children go to swell the sum of sufferings which was necessary to pay for truth, then I protest that the truth is not worth such a price. I don't want the mother to embrace the oppressor who threw her son to the dogs! She dare not forgive him! Let her forgive him for herself, if she will, let her forgive the torturer for the immeasurable suffering of her mother's heart. But the sufferings of her tortured child she has no right to forgive; she dare not forgive the torturer, even if the child were to forgive him! And if that is so, if they dare not forgive, what becomes of harmony? Is there in the whole world a being who would have the right to forgive and could forgive? I don't want harmony. From love for humanity I don't want it. I would rather be left with the unavenged suffering. I would rather remain with my unavenged suffering and unsatisfied indignation, *even if I were wrong.* Besides, too high a price is asked for harmony; it's beyond our means to pay so much to enter on it. And so I hasten to give back my entrance ticket, and if I am an honest man I am bound to give it back as soon as possible. And that I am doing. It's not God that I don't accept, Alyosha, only I most respectfully return Him the ticket."

"That's rebellion," murmured Alyosha, looking down.

"Rebellion? I am sorry you call it that," said Ivan earnestly. "One can hardly live in rebellion, and I want to live. Tell me yourself, I challenge you—answer. Imagine that you are creating a fabric of human destiny with the object of making men happy in the end, giving them peace and rest at last, but that it was essential and inevitable to torture to death only one tiny creature—that baby beating its breast with its fist, for instance—and to found that edifice on its unavenged tears, would you consent to be the architect on those conditions? Tell me, and tell the truth."

"No, I wouldn't consent," said Alyosha softly.

"And can you admit the idea that men for whom you are building it would agree to accept their happiness on the foundation of the unexpiated blood of a little victim? And accepting it would remain happy for ever?"

"No, I can't admit it. Brother," said Alyosha suddenly, with flashing eyes. "You said just now, is there a being in the whole world who would have the right to forgive and could forgive? But there is such a Being, and He can forgive everything, all and for all, because He gave His innocent blood for all and everything. You have forgotten Him, and on Him is built the edifice, and it is to Him they cry aloud, 'Thou art just, O Lord, for Thy ways are revealed!'"

"Ah! the One without sin and His blood! No, I have not forgotten Him; on the contrary I've been wondering all the time how it was you did not bring Him in before, for usually all arguments on your side put Him in the foreground. Do you know, Alyosha—don't laugh!—I made a poem about a year ago. If you can waste another ten minutes on me, I'll tell it to you."

"You wrote a poem?"

"Oh, no, I didn't write it," laughed Ivan, "and I've never written two lines of poetry in my life. But I made up this poem in prose and I remembered it. I was carried away when I made it up. You will be my first reader—that is, listener. Why should an author forego even one listener?" smiled Ivan. "Shall I tell it to you?"

"I am all attention," said Alyosha.

"My poem is called 'The Grand Inquisitor'; it's a ridiculous thing, but I want to tell it to you."

CHAPTER 5

The Grand Inquisitor

"Even this must have a preface—that is, a literary preface," laughed Ivan, "and I am a poor hand at making one. You see, my action takes place in the sixteenth century, and at that time, as you probably learnt at school, it was customary in poetry to bring down heavenly powers on earth. Not to speak of Dante, in France, clerks, as well as the monks in the monasteries, used to give regular performances in which the Madonna, the saints, the angels, Christ, and God Himself were brought on the stage. In those days it was done in all simplicity. In Victor Hugo's *Notre Dame de Paris* an edifying and gratuitous spectacle was provided for the people in the Hotel de Ville of Paris in the reign of Louis XI in honor of the birth of the dauphin. It was called *Le bon jugement de la très sainte et gracieuse Vierge Marie,** and she appears herself on the stage and pronounces her *bon jugement.* Similar plays, chiefly from the Old Testament, were occasionally performed in Moscow too, up to the times of Peter the Great. But besides plays there were all sorts of legends and ballads scattered about the world, in which the saints and angels and all the powers of Heaven took part when required. In our monasteries, the monks busied themselves in translating, copying, and even composing such poems—even under the Tatars. There is, for instance, one such poem (of course, from the Greek), 'The Wanderings of Our Lady through Hell,' with descriptions as bold as Dante's. Our Lady visits Hell, and the Archangel Michael leads her through the torments. She sees the sinners and their punishment. There she sees among others one noteworthy set of sinners in a burning lake; some of them sink to the bottom of the lake so that they can't swim out, and 'these God forgets'—an expression of extraordinary depth and force. And so Our Lady, shocked and weeping, falls before the throne of God and begs for mercy for all in Hell—for all she has seen there, and indiscriminately. Her conversation with God is immensely interesting. She beseeches Him; she will not desist; and when God points to the hands and feet of her Son,

*"The Merciful Judgment of the Very Saintly and Gracious Virgin Mary."

nailed to the Cross, and asks, 'How can I forgive His tormentors?' she
bids all the saints, all the martyrs, all the angels and archangels to fall
down with her and pray for mercy on all without distinction. It ends
by her winning from God a respite of suffering every year from Good
Friday till Trinity day, and the sinners at once raise a cry of thankful-
ness from Hell, chanting, 'Thou art just, O Lord, in this judgment.'
Well, my poem would have been of that kind if it had appeared at that
time. He comes on the scene in my poem, but He says nothing, only
appears and passes on. Fifteen centuries have passed since He promised to come in His glory, fifteen centuries since His prophet wrote,
'Behold, I come quickly.'* 'Of that day and that hour knoweth no man,
neither the Son, but the Father,' as He Himself predicted on earth.
But humanity awaits him with the same faith and with the same love.
Oh, with greater faith, for it is fifteen centuries since man has ceased
to see signs from Heaven.

> No signs from Heaven come today
> To add to what the heart doth say.

There was nothing left but faith in what the heart doth say. It is true
there were many miracles in those days. There were saints who performed miraculous cures; some holy people, according to their biog-
raphies, were visited by the Queen of Heaven herself. But the devil
did not slumber, and doubts were already arising among men of the
truth of these miracles. And just then there appeared in the north of
Germany a terrible new heresy. 'A huge star like to a torch' (that is, to
a church) 'fell on the sources of the waters and they became bitter.'
These heretics began blasphemously denying miracles. But those who
remained faithful were all the more ardent in their faith. The tears of
humanity rose up to Him as before, awaiting His coming, loved Him,
hoped for Him, yearned to suffer and die for Him as before. And so
many ages mankind had prayed with faith and fervor, 'O Lord our
God, hasten Thy coming,' so many ages called upon Him, that in His
infinite mercy He deigned to come down to His servants. Before that
day, He had come down; He had visited some holy men, martyrs and
hermits, as is written in their *Lives.* Among us, Tyutchev, with absolute faith in the truth of his words, bore witness that

*The Protestant Reformation and Catholic Counter-Reformation began with
Luther's act of protest in 1517.

> Bearing the Cross, in slavish dress
> Weary and worn, the Heavenly King
> Our mother, Russia, came to bless,
> And through our land went wandering.

And that certainly was so, I assure you.

"And behold, He deigned to appear for a moment to the people, to the tortured, suffering people, sunk in iniquity, but loving Him like children. My story is laid in Spain, in Seville, in the most terrible time of the Inquisition, when fires were lighted every day to the glory of God, and 'in the splendid *auto da fé*** the wicked heretics were burnt.' Oh, of course, this was not the coming in which He will appear according to His promise at the end of time in all His heavenly glory, and which will be sudden 'as lightning flashing from east to west.' No, He visited His children only for a moment, and there where the flames were crackling round the heretics. In His infinite mercy, He came once more among men in that human shape in which He walked among men for three years fifteen centuries ago. He came down to the 'hot pavement' of the southern town in which on the day before almost a hundred heretics had, *ad majorem gloriam Dei,*** been burnt by the cardinal, the Grand Inquisitor, in a magnificent *auto da fé,* in the presence of the king, the court, the knights, the cardinals, the most charming ladies of the court, and the whole population of Seville.

"He came softly, unobserved, and yet, strange to say, everyone recognized Him. That might be one of the best passages in the poem. I mean, why they recognized Him. The people are irresistibly drawn to Him; they surround Him; they flock about Him, follow Him. He moves silently in their midst with a gentle smile of infinite compassion. The sun of love burns in His heart, light and power shine from His eyes, and their radiance, shed on the people, stirs their hearts with responsive love. He holds out His hands to them, blesses them, and a healing virtue comes from contact with Him, even with His garments. An old man in the crowd, blind from childhood, cries out, 'O Lord, heal me and I shall see Thee!' and, as it were, scales fall from his eyes and the blind man sees Him. The crowd weeps and kisses the earth under His feet. Children throw flowers before Him,

---

*The public ceremony of judging and burning heretics during the Spanish Inquisition.
**"For the greater glory of God"—Jesuit motto.

sing, and cry hosannah. 'It is He—it is He!' all repeat. 'It must be He,
it can be no one but Him!' He stops at the steps of the Seville
cathedral at the moment when the weeping mourners are bringing in
a little open white coffin. In it lies a child of seven, the only daughter
of a prominent citizen. The dead child lies hidden in flowers. 'He will
raise your child,' the crowd shouts to the weeping mother. The priest,
coming to meet the coffin, looks perplexed and frowns, but the mother
of the dead child throws herself at His feet with a wail. 'If it is Thou,
raise my child!' she cries, holding out her hands to Him. The procession halts, the coffin is laid on the steps at His feet. He looks with
compassion, and His lips once more softly pronounce, 'Maiden, arise!'
and the maiden arises. The little girl sits up in the coffin and looks
round, smiling with wide-open wondering eyes, holding a bunch of
white roses they had put in her hand.

"There are cries, sobs, confusion among the people, and at that
moment the cardinal himself, the Grand Inquisitor, passes by the
cathedral. He is an old man, almost ninety, tall and erect, with a
withered face and sunken eyes, in which there is still a gleam of light.
He is not dressed in his gorgeous cardinal's robes, as he was the day
before, when he was burning the enemies of the Roman Church—at
that moment he is wearing his coarse, old monk's cassock. At a distance behind him come his gloomy assistant and slaves and the 'holy
guard.' He stops at the sight of the crowd and watches it from a
distance. He sees everything; he sees them set the coffin down at His
feet, sees the child rise up, and his face darkens. He knits his thick
grey brows and his eyes gleam with a sinister fire. He holds out his
finger and bids the guards take Him. And such is his power, so
completely are the people cowed into submission and trembling obedience to him, that the crowd immediately makes way for the guards,
and in the midst of deathlike silence they lay hands on Him and lead
Him away. The crowd instantly bows down to the earth, like one man,
before the old inquisitor. He blesses the people in silence and passes
on. The guards lead their prisoner to the close, gloomy, vaulted prison
in the ancient palace of the Holy Inquisition and shut Him in it. The
day passes and is followed by the dark, burning, 'breathless' night of
Seville. The air is 'fragrant with laurel and lemon.' In the pitch darkness, the iron door of the prison is suddenly opened and the Grand
Inquisitor himself comes in with a light in his hand. He is alone; the
door is closed at once behind him. He stands in the doorway and for a

minute or two gazes into His face. At last he goes up slowly, sets the light on the table, and speaks.

"'Is it Thou? Thou?' but receiving no answer, he adds at once, 'Don't answer; be silent. What canst Thou say, indeed? I know too well what Thou wouldst say. And Thou hast no right to add anything to what Thou hadst said of old. Why, then, art Thou come to hinder us? For Thou hast come to hinder us, and Thou knowest that. But dost Thou know what will be tomorrow? I know not who Thou art and care not to know whether it is Thou or only a semblance of Him, but tomorrow I shall condemn Thee and burn Thee at the stake as the worst of heretics. And the very people who have today kissed Thy feet, tomorrow at the faintest sign from me will rush to heap up the embers of Thy fire. Knowest Thou that? Yes, maybe Thou knowest it,' he added with thoughtful penetration, never for a moment taking his eyes off the Prisoner."

"I don't quite understand, Ivan. What does it mean?" Alyosha, who had been listening in silence, said with a smile. "Is it simply a wild fantasy, or a mistake on the part of the old man—some impossible *qui pro quo?*"*

"Take it as the last," said Ivan, laughing, "if you are so corrupted by modern realism and can't stand anything fantastic. If you like it to be a case of mistaken identity, let it be so. It is true," he went on, laughing, "the old man was ninety, and he might well be crazy over his set idea. He might have been struck by the appearance of the Prisoner. It might, in fact, be simply his ravings, the delusion of an old man of ninety, overexcited by the *auto da fé* of a hundred heretics the day before. But does it matter to us after all whether it was a mistake of identity or a wild fantasy? All that matters is that the old man should speak out, should speak openly of what he has thought in silence for ninety years."

"And the Prisoner too is silent? Does He look at him and not say a word?"

"That's inevitable in any case," Ivan laughed again. "The old man has told Him He hasn't the right to add anything to what He has said of old. One may say it is the most fundamental feature of Roman Catholicism, in my opinion at least. 'All has been given by Thee to the Pope,' they say, 'and all, therefore, is still in the Pope's hands, and

*Case of mistaken identity.

there is no need for Thee to come now at all. Thou must not meddle, for the time, at least.' That's how they speak and write too—the Jesuits, at any rate. I have read it myself in the works of their theologians. 'Hast Thou the right to reveal to us one of the mysteries of that world from which Thou hast come?' my old man asks Him, and answers the question for Him. 'No, Thou hast not; that Thou mayest not add to what has been said of old, and mayest not take from men the freedom which Thou didst exalt when Thou wast on earth. Whatsoever Thou revealest anew will encroach on men's freedom of faith, for it will be manifest as a miracle, and the freedom of their faith was dearer to Thee than anything in those days fifteen hundred years ago. Didst Thou not often say then, "I will make you free?" But now Thou hast seen these "free" men,' the old man adds suddenly, with a pensive smile. 'Yes, we've paid dearly for it,' he goes on, looking sternly at Him, 'but at last we have completed that work in Thy name. For fifteen centuries we have been wrestling with Thy freedom, but now it is ended and over for good. Dost Thou not believe that it's over for good? Thou lookest meekly at me and deignest not even to be wroth with me. But let me tell Thee that now, today, people are more persuaded than ever that they have perfect freedom, yet they have brought their freedom to us and laid it humbly at our feet. But that has been our doing. Was this what Thou didst? Was this Thy freedom?'"

"I don't understand again," Alyosha broke in. "Is he ironical? Is he jesting?"

"Not a bit of it! He claims it as a merit for himself and his Church that at last they have vanquished freedom and have done so to make men happy. 'For now' (he is speaking of the Inquisition, of course) 'for the first time it has become possible to think of the happiness of men. Man was created a rebel; and how can rebels be happy? Thou wast warned,' he says to Him. 'Thou hast had no lack of admonitions and warnings, but Thou didst not listen to those warnings; Thou didst reject the only way by which men might be made happy. But, fortunately, departing Thou didst hand on the work to us. Thou hast promised, Thou hast established by Thy word, Thou has given to us the right to bind and to unbind, and now, of course, Thou canst not think of taking it away. Why, then, hast Thou come to hinder us?'"

"And what's the meaning of 'no lack of admonitions and warnings'?" asked Alyosha.

"Why, that's the chief part of what the old man must say.

"'The wise and dread spirit, the spirit of self-destruction and nonexistence,' the old man goes on, 'the great spirit talked with Thee in the wilderness, and we are told in the books that he "tempted" Thee. Is that so? And could anything truer be said than what he revealed to Thee in three questions, and what Thou didst reject, and what in the books is called "the temptation"? And yet if there has ever been on earth a real, stupendous miracle, it took place on that day, on the day of the three temptations. The statement of those three questions was itself the miracle. If it were possible to imagine, simply for the sake of argument, that those three questions of the dread spirit had perished utterly from the books, and that we had to restore them and to invent them anew, and to do so had gathered together all the wise men of the earth—rulers, chief priests, learned men, philosophers, poets—and had set them the task to invent three questions, such as would not only fit the occasion, but express in three words, three human phrases, the whole future history of the world and of humanity—dost Thou believe that all the wisdom of the earth united could have invented anything in depth and force equal to the three questions which were actually put to Thee then by the wise and mighty spirit in the wilderness? From those questions alone, from the miracle of their statement, we can see that we have here to do not with the fleeting human intelligence, but with the absolute and eternal. For in those three questions the whole subsequent history of mankind is, as it were, brought together into one whole, and foretold, and in them are united all the unsolved historical contradictions of human nature. At the time, it could not be so clear, since the future was unknown; but now that fifteen hundred years have passed, we see that everything in those three questions was so justly divined and foretold, and has been so truly fulfilled, that nothing can be added to them or taken from them.

"'Judge Thyself who was right—Thou or he who questioned Thee then? Remember the first question; its meaning could be put this way: "Thou wouldst go into the world, and art going with empty hands, with some promise of freedom which men in their simplicity and their natural unruliness cannot even understand, which they fear and dread—for nothing has ever been more insupportable for a man and a human society than freedom. But seest Thou these stones in this parched and barren wilderness? Turn them into bread, and mankind will run after Thee like a flock of sheep, grateful and obedient, though forever trembling lest Thou withdraw Thy hand and deny them Thy bread." But Thou wouldst not deprive man of freedom, and didst reject the offer, thinking what is that freedom worth if obedience

is bought with bread? Thou didst reply that man lives not by bread
alone. But dost Thou know that for the sake of that earthly bread the
spirit of the earth will rise up against Thee and will strive with Thee
and overcome Thee, and all will follow him, crying, "Who can compare with this beast? He has given us fire from heaven!" Dost Thou
know that the ages will pass, and humanity will proclaim by the lips of
their sages that there is no crime, and therefore no sin; there is only
hunger? "Feed men, and then ask of them virtue!" that's what they'll
write on the bannner, which they will raise against Thee, and with
which they will destroy Thy temple. Where Thy temple stood will rise
a new building; the terrible tower of Babel will be built again, and
though, like the one of old, it will not be finished, yet Thou mightest
have prevented that new tower and have cut short the sufferings of
men for a thousand years; for they will come back to us after a
thousand years of agony with their tower. They will seek us again,
hidden underground in the catacombs, for we shall be again per-
secuted and tortured. They will find us and cry to us, "Feed us, for
those who have promised us fire from heaven haven't given it!" And
then we shall finish building their tower, for he finishes the building
who feeds them. And we alone shall feed them in Thy name, declaring
falsely that it is in Thy name. Oh, never, never can they feed themselves without us! No science will give them bread so long as they
remain free. In the end, they will lay their freedom at our feet, and say
to us, "Make us your slaves, but feed us." They will understand
themselves, at last, that freedom and bread enough for all are inconceivable together, for never, never will they be able to share between
them! They will be convinced, too, that they can never be free, for
they are weak, vicious, worthless, and rebellious. Thou didst promise
them the bread of Heaven, but, I repeat again, can it compare with
earthly bread in the eyes of the weak, ever sinful, and ignoble race of
man? And if for the sake of the bread of Heaven thousands and tens
of thousands shall follow Thee, what is to become of the millions and
tens of thousands of millions of creatures who will not have the
strength to forego the earthly bread for the sake of the heavenly? Or
dost Thou care only for the tens of thousands of the great and strong,
while the millions, numerous as the sands of the sea, who are weak
but love Thee, must exist only for the sake of the great and strong?
No, we care for the weak too. They are sinful and rebellious, but in
the end they too will become obedient. They will marvel at us and
look on us as gods, because we are ready to endure the freedom which

they have found so dreadful, and to rule over them—so awful it will seem to them to be free. But we shall tell them that we are Thy servants and rule them in Thy name. We shall deceive them again, for we will not let Thee come to us again. That deception will be our suffering, for we shall be forced to lie.

"'This is the significance of the first question in the wilderness, and this is what Thou hast rejected for the sake of that freedom which Thou hast exalted above everything. Yet in this question lies hidden the great secret of this world. Choosing "bread," Thou wouldst have satisfied the universal and everlasting craving of humanity—to find someone to worship. So long as man remains free, he strives for nothing so incessantly and so painfully as to find someone to worship. But man seeks to worship what is established beyond dispute, so that all men would agree at once to worship it. For these pitiful creatures are concerned not only to find what one or the other can worship, but to find something that all would believe in and worship; what is essential is that all may be *together* in it. This craving for *community* of worship is the chief misery of every man individually and of all humanity from the beginning of time. For the sake of common worship, they've slain each other with the sword. They have set up gods and challenged one another, "Put away your gods and come and worship ours, or we will kill you and your gods!" And so it will be to the end of the world, even when gods disappear from the earth; they will fall down before idols just the same. Thou didst know—Thou couldst not but have known—this fundamental secret of human nature, but Thou didst reject the one infallible banner that was offered Thee to make all men bow down to Thee alone—the banner of earthly bread; and Thou hast rejected it for the sake of freedom and the bread of Heaven. Behold what Thou didst further. And all again in the name of freedom! I tell Thee that man is tormented by no greater anxiety than to find someone quickly to whom he can hand over that gift of freedom with which the ill-fated creature is born. But only one who can appease their conscience can take over their freedom. In bread there was offered Thee an invincible banner; give bread, and man will worship Thee, for nothing is more certain than bread. But if someone else gains possession of his conscience—oh! then he will cast away Thy bread and follow after him who has ensnared his conscience. In that Thou wast right. For the secret of man's being is not only to live, but to have something to live for. Without a stable conception of the object of life, man would not consent to go on living, and would rather destroy himself than remain on earth, though he had bread in abundance. That is true. But what happened? Instead of taking men's freedom from them, Thou didst make it greater than ever! Didst Thou forget that man prefers peace, and even death, to freedom of choice in the knowledge of good and evil? Nothing is more seductive for man than his freedom of conscience, but nothing is a greater cause of suffering. And behold, instead of giving a firm foundation for setting the conscience of man at rest forever, Thou didst choose all that is exceptional, vague, and enigmatic; Thou didst choose what was utterly beyond the strength of men, acting as though Thou didst not love them at all—Thou, who didst come to give Thy life for them! Instead of taking possession of men's freedom, Thou didst increase it, and burdened the spiritual kingdom of mankind with its sufferings forever. Thou didst desire man's free love, that he should follow Thee freely, enticed and taken captive by Thee. In place of the rigid ancient law, man must hereafter, with free heart, decide for himself what is good and what is evil, having only Thy image before him as his guide. But didst Thou not know he would at last reject even Thy image and Thy truth, if he is weighed down with the fearful burden of free choice? They will cry aloud at last that the truth is not in Thee, for they could not have been left in greater confusion and suffering than Thou hast caused, laying upon them so many cares and unanswerable problems.

"'So that, in truth, Thou didst Thyself lay the foundation for the destruction of Thy kingdom, and no one is more to blame for it. Yet what was offered Thee? There are three powers, three powers alone, able to conquer and to hold captive forever the conscience of these impotent rebels for their happiness—those forces are miracle, mystery, and authority. Thou hast rejected all three, and hast set the example for doing so. When the wise and dread spirit set Thee on the pinnacle of the temple and said to Thee, "If Thou wouldst know whether Thou art the Son of God, then cast Thyself down, for it is written: the angels shall hold him up lest he fall and bruise himself, and Thou shalt know then whether Thou art the Son of God, and shalt prove then how great is Thy faith in Thy Father." But Thou didst refuse and wouldst not cast Thyself down. Oh, of course, Thou didst proudly and well, like God; but the weak, unruly race of men, are they gods? Oh, Thou didst know then that in taking one step, in making one movement to cast Thyself down, Thou wouldst be tempting God and have lost all Thy faith in Him, and wouldst have been dashed to pieces against that earth which Thou didst come to save.

And the wise spirit that tempted Thee would have rejoiced. But I ask again, are there many like Thee? And couldst Thou believe for one moment that men, too, could face such a temptation? Is the nature of men such, that they can reject miracle and at the great moments of their lives, the moments of their deepest, most agonizing spiritual difficulties, cling only to the free verdict of the heart? Oh, Thou didst know that Thy deed would be recorded in books, would be handed down to remote times and the utmost ends of the earth, and Thou didst hope that man, following Thee, would cling to God and not ask for a miracle. But Thou didst not know that, when man rejects miracle, he rejects God too; for man seeks not so much God as the miraculous. And as man cannot bear to be without the miraculous, he will create new miracles of his own for himself, and will worship deeds of sorcery and witchcraft, though he might be a hundred times over a rebel, heretic, and infidel. Thou didst not come down from the Cross when they shouted to Thee, mocking and reviling Thee, "Come down from the cross and we will believe that Thou art He." Thou didst not come down, for again Thou wouldst not enslave man by a miracle, and didst crave faith given freely, not based on miracle. Thou didst crave free love and not the base raptures of the slave before the might that has overawed him forever. But Thou didst think too highly of men therein, for they are slaves, of course, though rebellious by nature. Look around and judge; fifteen centuries have passed; look upon them. Whom hast Thou raised up to Thyself? I swear, man is weaker and baser by nature than Thou hast believed him! Can he, can he do what Thou didst? By showing him so much respect, Thou didst, as it were, cease to feel for him, for Thou didst ask far too much from him—Thou who hast loved him more than Thyself! Respecting him less, Thou wouldst have asked less of him. That would have been more like love, for his burden would have been lighter. He is weak and vile. What matter that he is everywhere now rebelling against our power, and proud of his rebellion? It is the pride of a child and a schoolboy. They are little children rioting and barring the teacher from school. But their childish delight will end; it will cost them dearly. They will cast down temples and drench the earth with blood. But they will see at last, the foolish children, that, though they are rebels, they are impotent rebels, unable to keep up their own rebellion. Bathed in their foolish tears, they will recognize at last that He who created them rebels must have meant to mock at them. They will say this in despair, and their utterance will be a blasphemy, which will make them more unhappy still, for man's nature cannot bear blasphemy, and in the end always gets revenge for it. And so unrest, confusion, and unhappiness—that is the present lot of man after Thou didst bear so much for their freedom! Thy great prophet tells in vision and in image that he saw all those who took part in the first resurrection, and that there were of each tribe twelve thousand.* But even if there were so many of them, they must have been not men, but gods. They had borne Thy cross; they had endured scores of years in the barren, hungry wilderness, living upon locusts and roots—and Thou mayest indeed point with pride at those children of freedom, of free love, of free and splendid sacrifice for Thy name. But remember that they were only some thousands; and what of the rest? And how are the other weak ones to blame, because they could not endure what the strong have endured? How is the weak soul to blame that it is unable to receive such terrible gifts? Canst Thou have simply come to the elect and for the elect? But if so, it is a mystery, and we cannot understand it. And if it is a mystery, we too have a right to preach a mystery, and to teach them that it's not the free judgment of their hearts, not love that matters, but a mystery which they must follow blindly, even against their conscience. So we have done. We have corrected Thy work and have founded it upon *miracle, mystery,* and *authority.* And men rejoiced that they were again led like sheep, and that the terrible gift that had brought them such suffering was, at last, lifted from their hearts. Were we right teaching them this? Speak! Did we not love mankind, so meekly acknowledging their feebleness, lovingly lightening their burden, and permitting their weak nature, even sin, with our sanction? Why hast Thou come now to hinder us? And why dost Thou look silently and searchingly at me with Thy mild eyes? Be angry. I don't want Thy love, for I love Thee not. And what use is it for me to hide anything from Thee? Don't I know to Whom I am speaking? All that I can say is known to Thee already. And is it for me to conceal from Thee our mystery? Perhaps it is Thy will to hear it from my lips. Listen, then. We are not working with Thee, but with *him*—that is our mystery. It's long—eight centuries—since we have been on *his* side and not on Thine. Just eight centuries ago, we took from him what Thou didst reject with scorn, that last gift he offered Thee, showing Thee all the kingdoms of the earth.** We took from

---

*According to the Revelation of St. John (7:4–8), 144,000 elect (12,000 from each of the twelve tribes) will achieve salvation at the end of time.

**Crucial events leading to the founding of the Holy Roman Empire and the

him Rome and the sword of Cæsar, and proclaimed ourselves sole rulers of the earth, though hitherto we have not been able to complete our work. But whose fault is that? Oh, the work is only beginning, but it has begun. It has long to await completion, and the earth has yet much to suffer, but we shall triumph and shall be Cæsars, and then we shall plan the universal happiness of man. But Thou mightest have taken even then the sword of Cæsar. Why didst Thou reject that last gift? Hadst Thou accepted that last counsel of the mighty spirit, Thou wouldst have accomplished all that man seeks on earth—that is, someone to worship, someone to keep his conscience, and some means of uniting all in one unanimous and harmonious ant-heap, for the craving for universal unity is the third and last anguish of men. Mankind as a whole has always striven to organize a universal state. There have been many great nations with great histories, but the more highly they were developed the more unhappy they were, for they felt more acutely than other people the craving for worldwide union. The great conquerors, Tamerlanes and Ghenghis-Khans, whirled like hurricanes over the face of the earth striving to subdue its people, and they too were but the unconscious expression of the same craving for universal unity. Hadst Thou taken the world and Cæsar's purple, Thou wouldst have founded the universal state and have given universal peace. For who can rule men if not he who holds their conscience and their bread in his hands? We have taken the sword of Cæsar, and in taking it, of course, have rejected Thee and followed *him*. Oh, ages are yet to come of the confusion of free thought, of their science and cannibalism. For having begun to build their tower of Babel without us, they will end, of course, with cannibalism. But then the beast will crawl to us and lick our feet and spatter them with tears of blood. And we shall sit upon the beast and raise the cup, and on it will be written, "Mystery." But then, and only then, the reign of peace and happiness will come for men. Thou art proud of Thine elect, but Thou hast only the elect, while we give rest to all. And, besides, how many of those elect, those mighty ones who could become elect, have grown weary waiting for Thee, and have transferred and will transfer the powers of their spirit and the warmth of their heart to the other camp, and end by raising their *free* banner against Thee. Thou didst Thyself lift up that banner. But, with us, all will be happy and will no longer rebel or destroy one another as under Thy freedom. Oh, we shall persuade

---

split between the Roman and Eastern Churches occurred in the late eighth century A.D.

them that they will only become free when they renounce their freedom to us and submit to us. And shall we be right or shall we be lying? They will be convinced that we are right, for they will remember the horrors of slavery and confusion to which Thy freedom brought them. Freedom, free thought, and science, will lead them into such straits and will bring them face to face with such marvels and insoluble mysteries, that some of them, the fierce and rebellious, will destroy themselves, others, rebellious but weak, will destroy one another, while the rest, weak and unhappy, will crawl fawning to our feet and whine to us: "Yes, you were right, you alone possess His mystery, and we come back to you, save us from ourselves!"

"'Receiving bread from us, they will see clearly that we take the bread made by their hands from them, to give it to them, without any miracle. They will see that we do not change the stones to bread, but in truth they will be more thankful for taking it from our hands than for the bread itself! For they will remember only too well that in old days, without our help, even the bread they made turned to stones in their hands, while, since they have come back to us, the very stones have turned to bread in their hands. Too, too well they know the value of complete submission! And until men know that, they will be unhappy. Who is most to blame for their not knowing it, speak? Who scattered the flock and sent it astray on unknown paths? But the flock will come together again and will submit once more, and then it will be once and for all. Then we shall give them the quiet, humble happiness of weak creatures such as they are by nature. Oh, we shall persuade them at last not to be proud, for Thou didst lift them up and thereby taught them to be proud. We shall show them that they are weak, that they are only pitiful children, but that childlike happiness is the sweetest of all. They will become timid, and will look to us and huddle close to us in fear, as chicks to the hen. They will marvel at us, and will be awestricken before us, and will be proud at our being so powerful and clever that we have been able to subdue such a turbulent flock of thousands of millions. They will tremble impotently before our wrath; their minds will grow fearful; they will be quick to shed tears like women and children; but they will be just as ready at a sign from us to pass to laughter and rejoicing, to happy mirth and childish song. Yes, we shall set them to work, but in their leisure hours we shall make their life like a child's game, with children's songs and innocent dance. Oh, we shall allow them even sin, they are weak and helpless, and they will love us like children because we allow them to sin. We shall tell them that every sin will be expiated, if it is done with our permission, that we allow them to sin because we love them, and the punishment for these sins we take upon ourselves. And we shall take it upon ourselves, and they will adore us as their saviors who have taken on themselves their sins before God. And they will have no secrets from us. We shall allow or forbid them to live with their wives and mistresses, to have or not to have children—according to whether they have been obedient or disobedient—and they will submit to us gladly and cheerfully. The most painful secrets of their conscience, all, all they will bring to us, and we shall have an answer for all. And they will be glad to believe our answer, for it will save them from the great anxiety and terrible agony they endure at present in making a free decision for themselves. And all will be happy, all the millions of creatures except the hundred thousand who rule over them. For only we, we who guard the mystery, shall be unhappy. There will be thousands of millions of happy babes, and a hundred thousand sufferers who have taken upon themselves the curse of the knowledge of good and evil. Peacefully they will die, peacefully they will expire in Thy name, and beyond the grave they will find nothing but death. But we shall keep the secret, and for their happiness we shall allure them with the reward of heaven and eternity. Though, if there were anything in the other world, it certainly would not be for such as they. It is prophesied that Thou wilt come again in victory; Thou wilt come with Thy chosen, the proud and strong. But we will say that they have only saved themselves, but we have saved all. We are told that the harlot who sits upon the beast and holds in her hands the *mystery* shall be put to shame, that the weak will rise up again, and will rend her royal purple and will strip naked her loathsome body. But then I will stand up and point out to Thee the thousand millions of happy children who have known no sin. And we who have taken their sins upon ourselves for their happiness will stand up before Thee and say, "Judge us if Thou canst and darest." Know that I fear Thee not. Know that I too have been in the wilderness, I too have lived on roots and locusts, I too prized the freedom with which Thou hast blessed men, and I too was striving to stand among Thy elect, among the strong and powerful, thirsting "to make up the number." But I awakened and would not serve madness. I turned back and joined the ranks of those *who have corrected Thy work*. I left the proud and went back to the humble, for the happiness of the humble. What I say to Thee will come to pass, and our dominion will be built up. I repeat, tomorrow Thou shalt see that obedient flock who at a sign from me will hasten to heap up the hot cinders about the pile on which I shall burn Thee for coming to hinder us. For if any one has ever deserved our fires, it is Thou. Tomorrow I shall burn Thee. *Dixi.*'"*

Ivan stopped. He was carried away as he talked and spoke with excitement; when he had finished, he suddenly smiled.

Alyosha had listened in silence; towards the end he was greatly moved and seemed several times on the point of interrupting, but restrained himself. Now his words came with a rush.

"But . . . that's absurd!" he cried, flushing. "Your poem is in praise of Jesus, not in blame of Him—as you meant it to be. And who will believe you about freedom? Is that the way to understand it? That's not the idea of it in the Orthodox Church . . . That's Rome, and not even the whole of Rome; it's false—those are the worst of the Catholics, the Inquisitors, the Jesuits! . . . And there could not be such a fantastic creature as your Inquisitor. What are these sins of mankind they take on themselves? Who are these keepers of the mystery who have taken some curse upon themselves for the happiness of mankind? When have they been seen? We know the Jesuits; they are spoken ill of, but surely they are not what you describe. They are not that at all, not at all. . . . They are simply the Romish army for the earthly sovereignty of the world in the future, with the Pontiff of Rome for Emperor . . . that's their ideal, but there's no sort of mystery or lofty melancholy about it. . . . It's simple lust for power, for filthy earthly gain, for domination—something like a universal serfdom with them as masters—that's all they stand for. They don't even believe in God perhaps. Your suffering inquisitor is a mere fantasy."

"Stay, stay," laughed Ivan. "How hot you are! A fantasy you say; let it be so! Of course it's a fantasy. But allow me to say, do you really think that the Roman Catholic movement of the last centuries is actually nothing but the lust for power, for filthy earthly gain? Is that Father Paissy's teaching?"

"No, no, on the contrary; Father Paissy did once say something rather the same as you . . . but, of course, it's not the same, not a bit the same," Alyosha hastily corrected himself.

"A precious admission, in spite of your 'not a bit the same.' I ask you why your Jesuits and Inquisitors have united simply for vile material gain? Why can there not be among them one martyr oppressed by

---

*I have spoken.

great sorrow and loving humanity? You see, only suppose that there was one such man among all those who desire nothing but filthy material gain—if there's only one like my old inquisitor, who had himself eaten roots in the desert and made frenzied efforts to subdue his flesh to make himself free and perfect. But yet all his life he loved humanity, and suddenly his eyes were opened, and he saw that it is no great moral blessedness to attain perfection and freedom, if at the same time one gains the conviction that millions of God's creatures have been created as a mockery, that they will never be capable of using their freedom, that these poor rebels can never turn into giants to complete the tower, that it was not for such geese that the great idealist dreamt his dream of harmony. Seeing all that, he turned back and joined—the clever people. Surely that could have happened?"

"Joined whom? What clever people?" cried Alyosha, completely carried away. "They have no such great cleverness and no mysteries and secrets. . . . Perhaps nothing but atheism, that's all their secret. Your inquisitor does not believe in God, that's his secret!"

"What if it is so! At last you have guessed it. It's perfectly true that that's the whole secret, but isn't that suffering, at least for a man like that, who has wasted his whole life in the desert and yet could not shake off his incurable love of humanity? In his old age, he reached the clear conviction that nothing but the advice of the great dread spirit could build up any tolerable sort of life for the feeble, unruly, 'incomplete, empirical creatures created in jest.' And so, convinced of this, he sees that he must follow the council of the wise spirit, the dread spirit of death and destruction, and therefore accept lying and deception, and lead men consciously to death and destruction, and yet deceive them all the way so that they may not notice where they are being led, that the poor blind creatures may at least on the way think themselves happy. And note, the deception is in the name of Him in Whose ideal the old man had so fervently believed all his life. Is not that tragic? And if only one such stood at the head of the whole army 'filled with the lust for power only for the sake of filthy gain'—would not one such be enough to make a tragedy? More than that, one such standing at the head is enough to create the actual leading idea of the Roman Church with all its armies and Jesuits, its highest idea. I tell you frankly that I firmly believe that there has always been such a man among those who stood at the head of the movement. Who knows, there may have been some such even among the Roman Popes. Who knows, perhaps the spirit of that accursed old man, who loves mankind so obstinately in his own way, is to be found even now in a whole multitude of such old men, existing not by chance but by agreement, as a secret league formed long ago for the guarding of the mystery, to guard it from the weak and the unhappy, so as to make them happy. No doubt it is so, and so it must be indeed. I fancy that even among the Masons there's something of the same mystery at the bottom, and that that's why the Catholics so detest the Masons as their rivals, breaking up the unity of the idea, while it is so essential that there should be one flock and one shepherd. . . . But from the way I defend my idea, I might be an author impatient of your criticism. Enough of it."

"You are perhaps a Mason yourself!" broke suddenly from Alyosha. "You don't believe in God," he added, speaking this time very sorrowfully. He fancied besides that his brother was looking at him ironically. "How does your poem end?" he asked, suddenly looking down. "Or was it the end?"

"I meant to end it like this. When the Inquisitor ceased speaking, he waited some time for his Prisoner to answer him. His silence weighed down upon him. He saw that the Prisoner had listened intently all the time, looking gently in his face and evidently not wishing to reply. The old man longed for Him to say something, however bitter and terrible. But He suddenly approached the old man in silence and softly kissed him on his bloodless, aged lips. That was all his answer. The old man shuddered. His lips moved. He went to the door, opened it, and said to Him, 'Go, and come no more. . . . Come not at all; never, never!' And he let Him out into the dark alleys of the town. The Prisoner went away."

"And the old man?"

"The kiss glows in his heart, but the old man adheres to his idea."

"And you with him, you too?" cried Alyosha, mournfully.

Ivan laughed.

"Why, it's all nonsense, Alyosha. It's only a senseless poem of a senseless student, who could never write two lines of verse. Why do you take it so seriously? Surely you don't suppose I am going straight off to the Jesuits, to join the men who are correcting His work? Good Lord, it's no business of mine. I told you, all I want is to live on to thirty, and then . . . dash the cup to the ground!"

"But the little sticky leaves, and the precious tombs, and the blue sky, and the woman you love! How will you live; how will you love them?" Alyosha cried sorrowfully. "With such a hell in your heart and your head, how can you? No, that's just what you are going away for, to join them . . . if not, you will kill yourself; you can't endure it!"

"There is a strength to endure everything," Ivan said with a cold smile.

"What strength?"

"The strength of the Karamazovs—the strength of the Karamazov baseness."

"To sink into debauchery, to stifle your soul with corruption, yes?"

"Possibly even that . . . only perhaps till I am thirty I shall escape it, and then."

"How will you escape it? By what will you escape it? That's impossible with your ideas."

"In the Karamazov way, again."

"'Everything is lawful,' you mean? Everything is lawful, is that it?"

Ivan scowled, and all at once turned strangely pale.

"Ah, you've picked up yesterday's phrase, which so offended Miusov—and which Dmitri pounced upon so naively and paraphrased!" he smiled queerly. "Yes, if you like, 'everything is lawful,' since the words have been said. I won't deny it."

Alyosha looked at him in silence.

"I thought that, going away from here, I have you at least," Ivan said suddenly, with unexpected feeling, "but now I see that there is no place for me even in your heart, my dear hermit. The formula, 'all is lawful,' I won't renounce—will you renounce me for that?"

Alyosha got up, went to him, and softly kissed him on the lips.

"That's plagiarism," cried Ivan, highly delighted. "You stole that from my poem. Thank you though. Get up, Alyosha, it's time we were going, both of us."

* * * * *

Book VI

The Russian Monk

Notes of the Life in God of the Deceased Priest
and Monk, the Elder Zossima,
Taken from His Own Words

BIOGRAPHICAL NOTES

(a) Father Zossima's Brother

Beloved fathers and teachers, I was born in a distant province in the north, in the town of V. My father was a gentleman by birth, but of no great consequence or position. He died when I was only two years old, and I don't remember him at all. He left my mother a small house built of wood, and an income, not large, but sufficient to keep her and her children in comfort. There were two of us, my elder brother Markel and I. He was eight years older than I was, of hasty, irritable temperament, but kind-hearted and never ironical. He was remarkably silent, especially at home with me, his mother, and the servants. He did well at school, but did not get on with his schoolfellows, though he never quarrelled, at least so my mother has told me. Six months before his death, when he was seventeen, he made friends with a political exile who had been banished from Moscow to our town for freethinking, and led a solitary existance there. He was a good scholar who had gained distinction in philosophy in the university. Something made him take a fancy to Markel, and he used to ask him to see him. The young man would spend whole evenings with him during that winter, until the exile was summoned to Petersburg to take up his post again at his own request, as he had powerful friends.

It was the beginning of Lent, and Markel would not fast; he was rude and laughed at it. "That's all silly twaddle and there is no God," he said, horrifying my mother, the servants, and me too. For though I was only nine, I too was aghast at hearing such words. We had four servants, all serfs. I remember my mother selling one of the four, the cook Afimya, who was lame and elderly, for sixty paper roubles, and hiring a free servant to take her place.

In the sixth week in Lent, my brother, who was never strong and had a tendency to consumption, was taken ill. He was tall but thin and delicate-looking, and of very pleasing countenance. I suppose he caught cold; anyway, the doctor who came soon whispered to my mother that it was galloping consumption, that he would not live through the spring. My mother began weeping, and careful not to alarm my brother she entreated him to go to church, to confess, and to take the sacrament, as he was still able to move about. This made him angry, and he said something profane about the church. He grew thoughtful, however; he guessed at once that he was seriously ill, and that that was why his mother was begging him to confess and take the sacrament. He had been aware, indeed, for a long time past that he was far from well, and had a year before coolly observed at dinner to our mother and me, "My life won't be long among you; I may not live another year," which seemed now like a prophecy.

Three days passed and Holy Week had come. And on Tuesday morning my brother began going to church. "I am doing this simply for your sake, mother, to please and comfort you," he said. My mother wept with joy and grief; "his end must be near," she thought, "if there's such a change in him." But he was not able to go to church long; he took to his bed, so he had to confess and take the sacrament at home.

It was a late Easter, and the days were bright, fine, and full of fragrance. I remember he used to cough all night and sleep badly, but in the morning he dressed and tried to sit up in an armchair. That's how I remember him sitting, sweet and gentle, smiling, his face bright and joyous, in spite of his illness. A marvellous change passed over him; his spirit seemed transformed. The old nurse would come in and say, "Let me light the lamp before the holy image, my dear." And once he would not have allowed it and would have blown it out.

"Light it, light it, dear, I was a wretch to have prevented you doing it. You are praying when you light the lamp, and I am praying when I rejoice seeing you. So we are praying to the same God."

Those words seemed strange to us, and mother would go to her room and weep, but when she went in to him she wiped her eyes and looked cheerful. "Mother, don't weep, darling," he would say, "I've long to live yet, long to rejoice with you, and life is glad and joyful."

"Ah, dear boy, how can you talk of joy when you lie feverish at night, coughing as though you would tear yourself to pieces."

"Don't cry, mother," he would answer, "life is paradise, and we are all in paradise, but we don't see it; if we did we should have heaven on earth the next day."

Every one wondered at his words; he spoke so strangely and positively; we were all touched and wept. Friends came to see us. "Dear ones," he would say to them, "what have I done that you should love me so; how can you love any one like me, and how was it I did not know, I did not appreciate it before?"

When the servants came in to him, he would say continually, "Dear, kind people, why are you doing so much for me; do I deserve to be waited on? If it were God's will for me to live, I would wait on you, for all men should wait on one another."

Mother shook her head as she listened. "My darling, it's your illness makes you talk like that."

"Mother darling," he would say, "there must be servants and masters, but if so I will be the servant of my servants, the same as they are to me. And another thing, mother, every one of us has sinned against all men, and I more than any."

Mother positively smiled at that and smiled through her tears. "Why, how could you have sinned against all men, more than all? Robbers and murderers have done that, but what sin have you committed yet that you hold yourself more guilty than all?"

"Mother, little heart of mine," he said (he had begun using such strange caressing words at that time), "little heart of mine, my joy, believe me, every one is really responsible to all men for all men and for everything. I don't know how to explain it to you, but I feel it is so, painfully even. And how is it we went on then living, getting angry and not knowing?"

So he would get up every day, more and more sweet and joyous and full of love. When the doctor, an old German called Eisenschmidt, came: "Well, doctor, have I another day in this world?" he would ask, joking.

"You'll live many days yet," the doctor would answer, "and months and years too."

"Months and years!" he would exclaim. "Why reckon the days? One day is enough for a man to know all happiness. My dear ones, why do we quarrel, try to outshine each other, and keep grudges against each other? Let's go straight into the garden, walk and play there, love, appreciate, and kiss each other, and glorify life."

"Your son cannot last long," the doctor told my mother, as she accompanied him to the door. "The disease is affecting his brain."

The windows of his room looked out into the garden, and our garden was a shady one, with old trees in it which were coming into bud. The first birds of spring were flitting in the branches, chirruping and singing at the windows. And looking at them and admiring them, he began suddenly begging their forgiveness too, "Birds of heaven, happy birds, forgive me, for I have sinned against you too." None of us could understand that at the time, but he shed tears of joy. "Yes," he said, "there was such a glory of God all about me; birds, trees, meadows, sky, only I lived in shame and dishonored it all and did not notice the beauty and glory."

"You take too many sins on yourself," mother used to say, weeping.

"Mother, darling, it's for joy, not for grief I am crying. Though I can't explain it to you, I like to humble myself before them, for I don't know how to love them enough. If I have sinned against everyone, yet all forgive me, too, and that's heaven. Am I not in heaven now?"

And there was a great deal more I don't remember. I remember I went once into his room when there was no one else there. It was a bright evening; the sun was setting, and the whole room was lighted up. He beckoned me, and I went up to him. He put his hands on my shoulders and looked into my face tenderly, lovingly; he said nothing for a minute, only looked at me like that.

"Well," he said, "run and play now, enjoy life for me too."

I went out then and ran to play. And many times in my life afterwards I remembered even with tears how he told me to enjoy life for him too. There were many other marvellous and beautiful sayings of his, though we did not understand them at the time. He died the third week after Easter. He was fully conscious, though he could not talk; up to his last hour he did not change. He looked happy; his eyes beamed and sought us; he smiled at us, beckoned us. There was a great deal of talk even in the town about his death. I was impressed by all this at the time, but not too much so, though I cried a great deal at his funeral. I was young then, a child; but a lasting impression, a hidden feeling of it all, remained in my heart, ready to rise up and respond when the time came. So indeed it happened.

(b) Of the Holy Scriptures in the life of Father Zossima

I was left alone with my mother. Her friends began advising her to send me to Petersburg as other parents did. "You have only one son now," they said, "and have a fair income, and you will be depriving him perhaps of a brilliant career if you keep him here." They suggested I should be sent to Petersburg to the Cadet Corps, that I might afterwards enter the Imperial Guard. My mother hesitated for a long time; it was awful to part with her only child, but she made up her mind to it at last, though not without many tears, believing she was acting for my happiness. She brought me to Petersburg and put me into the Cadet Corps, and I never saw her again. For she too died three years afterwards. She spent those three years mourning and grieving for both of us.

From the house of my childhood I have brought nothing but precious memories, for there are no memories more precious than those of early childhood in one's first home. And that is almost always so if there is any love and harmony in the family at all. Indeed, precious memories may remain even of a bad home, if only the heart knows how to find what is precious. With my memories of home I count, too, my memories of the Bible, which, child as I was, I was very eager to read at home. I had a book of Scripture history then with excellent pictures, called *A Hundred and Four Stories from the Old and New Testament,* and I learned to read from it. I have it lying on my shelf now; I keep it as a precious relic of the past. But even before I learned to read, I remember first being moved to devotional feeling at eight years old. My mother took me alone to mass (I don't remember where my brother was at the time) on the Monday before Easter. It was a fine day, and I remember today, as though I saw it now, how the incense rose from the censer and softly floated upwards and, overhead in the cupola, mingled in rising waves with the sunlight that streamed in at the little window. I was stirred by the sight, and for the first time in my life I consciously received the seed of God's word in my heart. A youth came out into the middle of the church carrying a big book, so large that at the time I fancied he could scarcely carry it. He laid it on the reading desk, opened it, and began reading, and suddenly for the first time I understood something read in the church of God. In the land of Uz, there lived a man, righteous and God-fearing, and he had great wealth, so many camels, so many sheep and asses, and his children feasted, and he loved them very much and prayed for them. "It may be that my sons have sinned in their feasting." Now the devil came before the Lord, together with the sons of God, and said to the Lord that he had gone up and down the earth and under the earth. "And hast thou considered my servant Job?" God asked of him. And God boasted to the devil, pointing to his great and holy servant. And the devil laughed at God's words. "Give him over to me and Thou wilt see that Thy servant will murmur against Thee and curse Thy name." And God gave up the just man He loved so, to the devil. And the devil smote his children and his cattle and scattered his wealth, all of a sudden like a thunderbolt from heaven. And Job rent his mantle and fell down upon the ground and cried aloud, "Naked came I out of my mother's womb, and naked shall I return into the earth; the Lord gave and the Lord has taken away. Blessed be the name of the Lord forever and ever."

Fathers and teachers, forgive my tears now, for all my childhood rises up again before me, and I breathe now as I breathed then, with the breast of a little child of eight, and I feel as I did then, awe and wonder and gladness. The camels at that time caught my imagination, and Satan, who talked like that with God, and God who gave His servant up to destruction, and His servant crying out, "Blessed be Thy name although Thou dost punish me," and then the soft and sweet singing in the Church, "Let my prayer rise up before Thee," and again incense from the priest's censer and the kneeling and the prayer. Ever since then—only yesterday I took it up—I've never been able to read that sacred tale without tears. And how much that is great, mysterious, and unfathomable there is in it! Afterwards I heard the words of mockery and blame, proud words: "How could God give up the most loved of His saints for the diversion of the devil, take from him his children, smite him with sore boils so that he cleansed the corruption from his sores with a potsherd—and for no object except to boast to the devil! 'See what My saint can suffer for My sake.'" But the greatness of it lies just in the fact that it is a mystery—that the passing earthly show and the eternal verity are brought together in it. In the face of the earthly truth, the eternal truth is accomplished. The Creator, just as on the first days of creation He ended each day with praise, "that is good that I have created," looks upon Job and again praises His creation. And Job, praising the Lord, serves not only Him but all His creation for generations and generations, and forever and ever, since for that he was ordained. Good heavens, what a book it is, and what lessons there are in it! What a book the Bible is; what a miracle; what strength is given with it to man. It is like a mould cast of the world and man and human nature; everything is there, and a law for everything for all the ages. And what mysteries are solved and revealed; God raises Job again, gives him wealth again. Many years pass by, and he has other children and loves them. But how could he

love those new ones when those first children are no more, when he
has lost them? Remembering them, how could he be fully happy with
those new ones, however dear the new ones might be? But he could,
he could. It's the great mystery of human life that old grief passes
gradually into quiet tender joy. The mild serenity of age takes the
place of the riotous blood of youth. I bless the rising sun each day and,
as before, my heart sings to meet it, but now I love even more its
setting, its long slanting rays and the soft tender gentle memories that
come with them, the dear images from the whole of my long happy
life—and over all the Divine Truth, softening, reconciling, forgiving!
My life is ending, I know that well, but every day that is left me I feel
how my earthly life is in touch with a new infinite, unknown, but
approaching life, the nearness of which sets my soul quivering with
rapture, my mind glowing and my heart weeping with joy.

Friends and teachers, I have heard more than once, and of late one
may hear it more often, that the priests, and above all the village
priests, are complaining on all sides of their miserable income and
their humiliating lot. They plainly state, even in print—I've read it
myself—that they are unable to teach the Scriptures to the people
because of the smallness of their means, and if Lutherans and heretics come and lead the flock astray, they let them lead them astray
because they have so little to live upon. May the Lord increase the
sustenance that is so precious to them, for their complaint is just, too.
But in truth I say, if anyone is to blame in the matter, half the fault is
ours. For he may be short of time, he may say truly that he is overwhelmed all the while with work and services, but still it's not all the
time; even he has an hour a week to remember God. And he does not
work the whole year round. Let him gather round him once a week,
some hour in the evening, if only the children at first—the fathers will
hear of it and they too will begin to come. There's no need to build
halls for this, let him take them into his own cottage. They won't spoil
his cottage; they only would be there one hour. Let him open that
book and begin reading it, without grand words or superciliousness,
without condescension to them, but gently and kindly, being glad that
he is reading to them and that they are listening with attention, loving
the words himself, only stopping from time to time to explain words
that are not understood by the peasants. Don't be anxious; they will
understand everything; the orthodox heart will understand all! Let
him read to them about Abraham and Sarah, about Isaac and Re-
becca, of how Jacob went to Laban and wrestled with the Lord in his

dream and said, "This place is holy"—and he will impress the devout mind of the peasant. Let him read, especially to the children, how the brothers sold Joseph, the tender boy, the dreamer and prophet, into bondage, and told their father that a wild beast had devoured him, and showed him his blood-stained clothes. Let him read to them how the brothers afterwards journeyed into Egypt for corn, and Joseph, already a great ruler, unrecognized by them, tormented them, accused them, kept his brother Benjamin, and all through love: "I love you, and loving you I torment you." For he remembered all his life how they had sold him to the merchants in the burning desert by the well, and how, wringing his hands, he had wept and besought his brothers not to sell him as a slave in a strange land. And how, seeing them again after many years, he loved them beyond measure, but he harassed and tormented them in love. He left them at last and, not able to bear the suffering of his heart, flung himself on his bed and wept. Then, wiping his tears away, he went out to them joyfully and told them, "Brothers, I am your brother Joseph!" Let him read to them further how happy old Jacob was on learning that his darling boy was still alive, and how he went to Egypt, leaving his own country, and died in a foreign land, bequeathing his great prophecy that had lain mysteriously hidden in his meek and timid heart all his life, that from his offspring, from Judah, will come the great hope of the world, the Messiah and Saviour.

Fathers and teachers, forgive me and don't be angry, that like a little child I've been babbling of what you have long known and can teach me a hundred times more skilfully. I only speak from rapture, and forgive my tears, for I love the Bible. Let him too weep, the priest of God, and be sure that the hearts of his listeners will throb in response. Only a little tiny seed is needed—drop it into the heart of the peasant and it won't die, it will live in his soul all his life; it will be hidden in the midst of his darkness and sin, like a bright spot, like a great reminder. And there's no need of much teaching or explanation; he will understand it all simply. Do you suppose that the peasants don't understand? Try reading them the touching story of the fair Esther and the haughty Vashti; or the miraculous story of Jonah in the whale. Don't forget, either, the parables of Our Lord; choose especially from the Gospel of St. Luke (that is what I did), and then, from the Acts of the Apostles, the conversion of St. Paul (that you mustn't leave out on any account), and from the *Lives of the Saints*, for instance, the life of Alexey, the man of God and, greatest of all, the happy martyr and the seer of God, Mary of Egypt—and you will penetrate their hearts with these simple tales. Give one hour a week to it in spite of your poverty, only one little hour. And you will see for yourself that our people are gracious and grateful, and will repay you a hundredfold. Mindful of the kindness of their priest and the moving words they have heard from him, they will of their own accord help him in his fields and in his house, and will treat him with more respect than before—so that it will even increase his worldly well being too. The thing is so simple that sometimes one is even afraid to put it into words for fear of being laughed at, and yet how true it is! One who does not believe in God will not believe in God's people. He who believes in God's people will see His Holiness too, even though he had not believed in it till then. Only the people and their future spiritual power will convert our atheists, who have torn themselves away from their native soil.

And what is the use of Christ's words unless we set an example? The people are lost without the word of God, for their souls are athirst for the Word and for all that is good.

In my youth, long ago, nearly forty years ago, I traveled all over Russia with Father Anfim collecting funds for our monastery, and we stayed one night on the bank of a great navigable river with some fishermen. A good-looking peasant lad, about eighteen, joined us; he had to hurry back next morning to pull a merchant's barge along the bank. I noticed him looking straight before him with clear and tender eyes. It was a bright, warm, still, July night; a cool mist rose from the broad river; we could hear the splash of a fish; the birds were still; all was hushed and beautiful, everything praying to God. Only we two were not sleeping, the lad and I, and we talked of the beauty of this world of God's and of the great mystery of it. Every blade of grass, every insect, ant, and golden bee, all so marvellously know their path, though they have not intelligence; they bear witness to the mystery of God and continually accomplish it themselves. I saw the dear lad's heart was moved. He told me that he loved the forest and the forest birds. He was a birdcatcher, knew the note of each of them, could call each bird. "I know nothing better than to be in the forest," said he, "though all things are good."

"Truly," I answered him, "all things are good and fair, because all is truth. Look," said I, "at the horse, that great beast that is so near to man; or the lowly, pensive ox, which feeds him and works for him; look at their faces; what meekness, what devotion to man, who often

beats them mercilessly. What gentleness, what confidence, and what
beauty! It's touching to know that there's no sin in them, for all, all
except man, is sinless, and Christ has been with them before us."

"Why," asked the boy, "is Christ with them too?"

"It cannot but be so," said I, "since the Word is for all. All creation
and all creatures, every leaf is striving to the Word, singing glory to
God, weeping to Christ, unconsciously accomplishing this by the
mystery of their sinless life. Yonder," said I, "in the forest wanders the
dreadful bear, fierce and menacing, and yet innocent in it." And I told
him how once a bear came to a great saint who had taken refuge in a
tiny cell in the wood. "And the great saint pitied him, went up to him
without fear and gave him a piece of bread. 'Go along,' said he,
'Christ be with you,' and the savage beast walked away meekly and
obediently, doing no harm." And the lad was delighted that the bear
had walked away without hurting the saint, and that Christ was with
him too. "Ah," said he, "how good that is. How good and beautiful is
all God's work!" He sat musing softly and sweetly. I saw he understood. And he slept beside me a light and sinless sleep. May God bless
youth! And I prayed for him as I went to sleep. Lord, send peace and
light to Thy people!

(c) Recollections of Father Zossima's youth
before he became a monk. The duel

I spent a long time, almost eight years, in the military cadet school
at Petersburg, and in the novelty of my surroundings there, many of
my childish impressions grew dimmer, though I forgot nothing. I
picked up so many new habits and opinions that I was transformed
into a cruel, absurd, almost savage creature. A surface polish of cour-
tesy and society manners I did acquire together with the French
language.

But we all, myself included, looked upon the soldiers in our service
as cattle. I was perhaps worse than the rest in that respect, for I was so
much more impressionable than my companions. By the time we left
the school as officers, we were ready to lay down our lives for the
honor of the regiment, but no one of us had any knowledge of the real
meaning of honor, and if any one had known it, he would have been
the first to ridicule it. Drunkenness, debauchery, and devilry were
what we prided ourselves on. I don't say that we were bad by nature; all
these young men were good fellows, but they behaved badly, and I

worst of all. What made it worse for me was that I had come into my own money, and so I flung myself into a life of pleasure, and plunged headlong into all the recklessness of youth.

I was fond of reading, yet strange to say the Bible was the one book I never opened at that time, though I always carried it about with me, and I was never separated from it; in very truth I was keeping that book "for the day and the hour, for the month and the year," though I did not know it.

After four years of this life, I chanced to be in the town of K. where our regiment was stationed at the time. We found the people of the town hospitable, rich, and fond of entertainments. I met with a cordial reception everywhere, as I was of a lively temperament and was known to be well off, which always goes a long way in the world. And then a circumstance happened which was the beginning of it all.

I formed an attachment to a beautiful and intelligent young girl of noble and lofty character, the daughter of people much respected. They were well-to-do people of influence and position. They always gave me a cordial and friendly reception. I fancied that the young lady looked on me with favor and my heart was aflame at such an idea. Later on I saw and fully realized that I perhaps was not so passionately in love with her at all, but only recognized the elevation of her mind and character, which I could not indeed have helped doing. I was prevented, however, from making her an offer at the time by my selfishness; I was loath to part with the allurements of my free and licentious bachelor life in the heyday of my youth, and with my pockets full of money. I did drop some hint as to my feelings, however, though I put off taking any decisive step for a time. Then, all of a sudden, we were ordered off for two months to another district.

On my return two months later, I found the young lady already married to a rich neighboring landowner, a very amiable man, still young, though older than I was, connected with the best Petersburg society, which I was not, and of excellent education, which I also was not. I was so overwhelmed at this unexpected circumstance that my mind was positively clouded. The worst of it all was that, as I learned then, the young landowner had been a long while betrothed to her, and I had met him indeed many times in her house, but blinded by my conceit I had noticed nothing. And this particularly mortified me; almost everybody had known all about it, while I knew nothing. I was filled with sudden, irrepressible fury. With flushed face, I began recalling how often I had been on the point of declaring my love to her, and as she had not attempted to stop me or to warn me, she must, I concluded, have been laughing at me all the time. Later on, of course, I reflected and remembered that she had been very far from laughing at me; on the contrary, she used to turn off any courting on my part with a joke and begin talking of other subjects; but at that moment I was incapable of reflecting and was all eagerness for revenge. I am surprised to remember that my wrath and revengeful feelings were extremely repugnant to my own nature, for being of an easy temper, I found it difficult to be angry with anyone for long, and so I had to work myself up artificially and became at last revolting and absurd.

I waited for an opportunity and succeeded in insulting my "rival" in the presence of a large company. I insulted him on a perfectly extraneous pretext, jeering at his opinion upon an important public event—it was in the year 1826*—and my jeer was, so people said, clever and effective. Then I forced him to ask for an explanation, and behaved so rudely that he accepted my challenge in spite of the vast inequality between us, as I was younger, a person of no consequence, and of inferior rank. I learned afterwards for a fact that it was from a jealous feeling on his side also that my challenge was accepted; he had been rather jealous of me on his wife's account before their marriage; he fancied now that if he submitted to being insulted by me and refused to accept any challenge, and if she heard of it, she might begin to despise him and waver in her love for him. I soon found a second in a comrade, an ensign of our regiment. In those days, though duels were severely punished, yet duelling was a kind of fashion among the officers—so strong and deeply rooted will a brutal prejudice sometimes be.

It was the end of June, and our meeting was to take place at seven o'clock the next day on the outskirts of the town—and then something happened that in very truth was the turning-point of my life. In the evening, returning home in a savage and brutal humor, I flew into a rage with my orderly, Afanasy, and gave him two blows in the face with all my might, so that it was covered with blood. He had not long been in my service and I had struck him before, but never with such ferocious cruelty. And, believe me, though it's forty years ago, I recall it now with shame and pain. I went to bed and slept for about three

---

*Probably the Decembrist plot against the Tsar in 1825 in which the most distinguished men in Russia were concerned.

hours; when I woke up, the day was breaking. I got up—I did not want
to sleep any more—I went to the window—opened it; it looked out
upon the garden; I saw the sun rising; it was warm and beautiful; the
birds were singing.

What's the meaning of it, I thought? I feel in my heart something
vile and shameful. Is it because I am going to shed blood? No, I
thought, I feel it's not that. Can it be that I am afraid of death, afraid of
being killed? No, that's not it, that's not it at all . . . And all at once I
knew what it was: it was because I had beaten Afanasy the evening
before! It all rose before my mind; it all was, as it were, repeated over
again; he stood before me and I was beating him straight on the face
and he was holding his arms stiffly down, his head erect, his eyes fixed
upon me as though on parade. He staggered at every blow and did not
even dare to raise his hands to protect himself. That is what a man has
been brought to, and that was a man beating a fellow creature! What a
crime! It was as though a sharp dagger had pierced me right through.
I stood as if I were struck dumb, while the sun was shining, the leaves
were rejoicing and the birds were trilling the praise of God . . . I hid
my face in my hands, fell on my bed, and broke into a storm of tears.
And then I remembered my brother Markel and what he said on his
deathbed to his servants: "My dear ones, why do you wait on me, why
do you love me, am I worth your waiting on me?"

Yes, am I worth it? flashed through my mind. After all, what am I
worth that another man, a fellow creature, made in the likeness and
image of God, should serve me? For the first time in my life this
question forced itself upon me. He had said, "Mother, my little heart,
in truth we are each responsible to all for all, it's only that men don't
know this. If they know it, the world would be a paradise at once."

"God, can that too be false?" I thought as I wept. "In truth, perhaps, I am more than all others responsible for all, a greater sinner
than all men in the world." And all at once the whole truth in its full
light appeared to me: what was I going to do? I was going to kill a
good, clever, noble man, who had done me no wrong, and by depriving his wife of happiness for the rest of her life, I should be torturing
and killing her too. I lay thus in my bed with my face in the pillow,
heedless how the time was passing. Suddenly my second, the ensign,
came in with the pistols to fetch me.

"Ah," said he, "it's a good thing you are up already; it's time we
were off; come along!"

I did not know what to do and hurried to and fro undecidedly; we went out to the carriage, however.

"Wait here a minute," I said to him. "I'll be back directly; I have forgotten my wallet."

And I ran back alone, straight to Afanasy's little room.

"Afanasy," I said, "I gave you two blows on the face yesterday; forgive me," I said.

He started as though he were frightened, and looked at me; and I saw that it was not enough, and on the spot, in my full officer's uniform, I dropped at his feet and bowed my head to the ground.

"Forgive me," I said.

Then he was completely aghast.

"Your honor . . . sir, what are you doing? Am I worth it?"

And he burst out crying as I had done before, hid his face in his hands, turned to the window, and shook all over with his sobs. I flew out to my comrade and jumped into the carriage.

"Ready," I cried. "Have you ever seen a conqueror?" I asked him. "Here is one before you."

I was in ecstasy, laughing and talking all the way; I don't remember what about.

He looked at me. "Well, brother, you are a plucky fellow, you'll keep up the honor of the uniform, I can see."

So we reached the place and found them there, awaiting us. We were placed twelve paces apart; he had the first shot. I stood gaily, looking him full in the face; I did not twitch an eyelash. I looked lovingly at him, for I knew what I would do. His shot just grazed my cheek and ear.

"Thank God," I cried, "no man has been killed," and I seized my pistol, turned back, and flung it far into the wood.

"That's the place for you," I cried.

I turned to my adversary.

"Forgive me, young fool that I am, sir," I said, "for my unprovoked insult to you and for forcing you to fire at me. I am ten times worse than you and more, maybe. Tell that to the person whom you hold dearest in the world."

I had no sooner said this than all three shouted at me.

"Upon my word," cried my adversary, annoyed, "if you did not want to fight, why didn't you leave me alone?"

"Yesterday I was a fool; today I know better," I answered him gaily.

"As to yesterday, I believe you, but as for today, it is difficult to agree with your opinion," said he.

"Bravo," I cried, clapping my hands. "I agree with you there too; I have deserved it!"

"Will you shoot, sir, or not?"

"No, I won't," I said, "if you like, fire at me again, but it would be better for you not to fire."

The seconds, especially mine, were shouting too: "Can you disgrace the regiment like this, facing your antagonist and begging his forgiveness! If I'd only known this!"

I stood facing them all, not laughing now.

"Gentlemen," I said, "is it really so wonderful in these days to find a man who can repent of his stupidity and publicly confess his wrongdoing?"

"But not in a duel," cried my second again.

"That's what's so strange," I said. "For I ought to have owned my fault as soon as I got here, before he had fired a shot, before leading him into a great and deadly sin; but we have made our life so grotesque, that to act in that way would have been almost impossible, for only after I have faced his shot at the distance of twelve paces could my words have any significance for him, and if I had spoken before, he would have said 'he is a coward, the sight of the pistols had frightened him, no use to listen to him.' Gentlemen," I cried suddenly, speaking straight from my heart, "look around you at the gifts of God, the clear sky, the pure air, the tender grass, the birds; nature is beautiful and sinless, and we, only we, are sinful and foolish, and we don't understand that life is heaven, for we have only to understand that and it will at once be fulfilled in all its beauty, we shall embrace each other and weep."

I would have said more but I could not; my voice broke with the sweetness and youthful gladness of it, and there was such bliss in my heart as I had never known before in my life.

"All this is rational and edifying," said my antagonist, "and in any case you are an original person."

"You may laugh," I said to him, laughing too, "but afterwards you will approve of me."

"Oh, I am ready to approve of you now," said he; "will you shake hands, for I believe you are genuinely sincere."

"No," I said, "not now; later on when I have grown worthier and deserve your esteem, then shake hands and you will do well."

We went home, my second upbraiding me all the way, while I kissed him. All my comrades heard of the affair at once and gathered together to pass judgment on me the same day.

"He has disgraced the uniform," they said; "let him resign his commission."

Some stood up for me: "He faced the shot," they said.

"Yes, but he was afraid of his other shot and begged for forgiveness."

"If he had been afraid of being shot, he would have shot his own pistol first before asking forgiveness, but he flung it loaded into the forest. No, there's something else in this, something original."

I enjoyed listening and looking at them. "My dear friends and comrades," said I, "don't worry about my resigning my commission, for I have done so already. I have sent in my papers this morning and as soon as I get my discharge, I shall go into a monastery—it's with that object I am leaving the regiment."

When I had said this every one of them burst out laughing.

"You should have told us of that first; that explains everything; we can't judge a monk."

They laughed and could not stop themselves, and not scornfully, but kindly and merrily. They all felt friendly to me at once, even those who had been sternest in their censure, and all the following month, before my discharge came, they could not make enough of me. "Ah, you monk," they would say. And everyone said something kind to me; they began trying to dissuade me, even to pity me: "What are you doing to yourself?"

"No," they would say, "he is a brave fellow, he faced fire and could have fired his own pistol too, but he had a dream the night before that he should become a monk; that's why he did it."

It was the same thing with the society of the town. Until then I had been kindly received, but had not been the object of special attention. But now all came to know me at once and invited me; they laughed at me, but they loved me. I may mention that although everybody talked openly of our duel, the authorities took no notice of it, because my antagonist was a near relation of our general, and, as there had been no bloodshed and no serious consequences, and as I resigned my commission, they took it as a joke. And I began then to speak aloud and fearlessly, regardless of their laughter, for it was always kindly and not spiteful laughter. These conversations mostly took place in the evenings, in the company of ladies; women particularly liked listening to me then, and they made the men listen.

"But how can I possibly be responsible for all?" everyone would laugh in my face. "Can I, for instance, be responsible for you?"

"You may well not know it," I would answer, "since the whole world has long been going on a different line, since we consider the veriest lies as truth and demand the same lies from others. Here I have for once in my life acted sincerely and, well, you all look upon me as a madman. Though you are friendly to me, yet, you see, you all laugh at me."

"But how can we help being friendly to you?" said my hostess, laughing. The room was full of people. All of a sudden the young lady rose, on whose account the duel had been fought and whom only lately I had intended to be my future wife. I had not noticed her coming into the room. She got up, came to me, and held out her hand.

"Let me tell you," she said, "that I am the first not to laugh at you, but on the contrary I thank you with tears and express my respect for you and for your action then."

Her husband too came up and then they all approached me and almost kissed me. My heart was filled with joy, but my attention was especially caught by a middle-aged man who came up to me with the others. I knew him by name already, but had never made his acquaintance nor exchanged a word with him until that evening.

(d) The mysterious visitor

He had long been an official in the town; he was in a prominent position, respected by all, rich, and with a reputation for benevolence. He subscribed considerable sums to the almshouse and the orphan asylum; he was very charitable, too, in secret, a fact which only became known after his death. He was about fifty, almost stern in appearance, and not much given to conversation. He had been married about ten years and his wife, who was still young, had borne him three children. Well, I was sitting alone in my room the following evening when my door suddenly opened and this gentleman walked in.

I must mention, by the way, that I was no longer living in my former quarters. As soon as I resigned my commission, I took rooms with an old lady, the widow of a government clerk. My landlady's servant waited upon me, for I had moved into her rooms simply because on my return from the duel I had sent Afanasy back to the regiment, as I felt ashamed to look him in the face after my last meeting with him. So prone is the man of the world to be ashamed of any righteous action.

"I have," said my visitor, "with great interest listened to you speaking in different houses the last few days, and I wanted at last to make your personal acquaintance so as to talk to you more intimately. Can you, dear sir, grant me this favor?"

"I can, with the greatest pleasure, and I shall look upon it as an honor." I said this, though I felt almost dismayed, so greatly was I impressed from the first moment by the appearance of this man. For though other people had listened to me with interest and attention, no one had come to me before with such a serious, stern, and concentrated expression. And now he had come to see me in my rooms. He sat down.

"You are, I see, a man of great strength of character," he said, "as you have dared to serve the truth, even when by doing so you risked incurring the contempt of all."

"Your praise is, perhaps, excessive," I replied.

"No, it's not excessive," he answered; "believe me, such a course of action is far more difficult than you think. It is that which has impressed me, and it is only on that account that I have come to you," he continued. "Tell me, please, that is if you are not annoyed by my perhaps unseemly curiosity, what were your exact sensations, if you can recall them, at the moment when you made up your mind to ask forgiveness at the duel? Do not think my question frivolous; on the contrary, I have in asking the question a secret motive of my own, which I will perhaps explain to you later on, if it is God's will that we should become more intimately acquainted."

All the while he was speaking, I was looking at him straight in the face, and I felt all at once a complete trust in him, and great curiosity on my side also, for I felt that there was some strange secret in his soul.

"You ask what were my exact sensations at the moment when I asked my opponent's forgiveness," I answered. "But I had better tell you from the beginning what I have not yet told anyone else." And I described all that had passed between Afanasy and me, and how I had bowed down to the ground at his feet. "From that you can see for yourself," I concluded, "that at the time of the duel it was easier for me, for I had made a beginning already at home, and when once I had started on the road, to go further along it was far from being difficult, but became a source of joy and happiness."

I liked the way he looked at me as he listened. "All that," he said, "is exceedingly interesting. I will come to see you again and again."

And from that time forth he came to see me nearly every evening. And we should have become greater friends, if only he had ever talked of himself. But about himself he scarcely ever said a word, yet continually asked me about myself. In spite of that, I became very fond of him, and spoke with perfect frankness to him about all my feelings; for, thought I, what need have I to know his secrets, since I can see without that that he is a good man. Moreoever, though he is such a serious man and my senior, he comes to see a youngster like me and treats me as his equal. And I learned a great deal that was profitable from him, for he was a man of lofty mind.

"That life is heaven," he said to me suddenly, "that I have long been thinking about;" and all at once he added, "I think of nothing else indeed." He looked at me and smiled. "I am more convinced of it than you are; I will tell you later why."

I listened to him and thought that he evidently wanted to tell me something.

"Heaven," he went on, "lies hidden within all of us—here it lies hidden in me now, and if I will it, it will be revealed to me tomorrow and for all time."

I looked at him; he was speaking with great emotion and gazing mysteriously at me, as if he were questioning me.

"And that we are all responsible to all for all, apart from our own sins, you were quite right in thinking that, and it is wonderful how you could comprehend it in all its significance at once. And in very truth, so soon as men understand that, the Kingdom of Heaven will be for them not a dream, but a living reality."

"And when," I cried out to him bitterly, "when will that come to pass? And will it ever come to pass? Is it not simply a dream of ours?"

"What, then, you don't believe it?" he said. "You preach it and don't believe it yourself. Believe me; this dream, as you call it, will come to pass without doubt; it will come, but not now, for every process has its law. It's a spiritual, psychological process. To transform the world, to recreate it afresh, men must turn into another path psychologically. Until you have become really, in actual fact, a brother to everyone, brotherhood will not come to pass. No sort of scientific teaching, no kind of common interest, will ever teach men to share property and privileges with equal consideration for all. Everyone will think his share too small, and they will be always envying, complaining, and attacking one another. You ask when it will come to pass; it will come to pass, but first we have to go through the period of isolation."

"What do you mean by isolation?" I asked him.

"Why, the isolation that prevails everywhere, above all in our age—it has not fully developed, it has not reached its limit yet. For everyone strives to keep his individuality as apart as possible, wishes to secure the greatest possible fulness of life for himself; but meantime all his efforts result not in attaining fulness of life but in self-destruction, for instead of self-realization, he ends by arriving at complete solitude. All mankind in our age have split up into units; they all keep apart, each in his own groove; each one holds aloof, hides himself and hides what he has, from the rest, and he ends by being repelled by others and repelling them. He heaps up riches by himself and thinks, 'How strong I am now and how secure,' and in his madness he does not understand that the more he heaps up, the more he sinks into self-destructive impotence. For he is accustomed to rely upon himself alone and to cut himself off from the whole; he has trained himself not to believe in the help of others, in men and in humanity, and only trembles for fear he should lose his money and the privileges that he has won for himself. Everywhere in these days men have, in their mockery, ceased to understand that the true security is to be found in social solidarity rather than in isolated individual effort. But this terrible individualism must inevitably have an end, and all will suddenly understand how unnaturally they are separated from one another. It will be the spirit of the time, and people will marvel that they have sat so long in darkness without seeing the light. And then the sign of the Son of Man will be seen in the heavens. . . . But, until then, we must keep the banner flying. Sometimes even if he has to do it alone, and his conduct seems to be crazy, a man must set an example, and so draw men's souls out of their solitude, and spur them to some act of brotherly love, that the great idea may not die."

Our evenings, one after another, were spent in such stirring and fervent talk. I gave up society and visited my neighbors much less frequently. Besides, my vogue was somewhat over. I say this, not as blame, for they still loved me and treated me good-humoredly, but there's no denying that fashion is a great power in society. I began to regard my mysterious visitor with admiration, for besides enjoying his intelligence, I began to perceive that he was brooding over some plan in his heart, and was preparing himself perhaps for a great deed. Perhaps he liked my not showing curiosity about his secret, not seeking to discover it by direct question nor by insinuation. But I noticed, at last, that he seemed to show signs of wanting to tell me something. This had become quite evident, indeed, about a month after he first began to visit me.

"Do you know," he said to me once, "that people are very inquisitive about us in the town and wonder why I come to see you so often. But let them wonder, for *soon all will be explained.*"

Sometimes an extraordinary agitation would come over him, and almost always on such occasions he would get up and go away. Sometimes he would fix a long piercing look upon me, and I thought, "He will say something directly now." But he would suddenly begin talking of something ordinary and familiar. He often complained of headache too.

One day, quite unexpectedly indeed, after he had been talking with great fervor a long time, I saw him suddenly turn pale, and his face worked convulsively, while he stared persistently at me.

"What's the matter?" I said; "do you feel ill?"—he had just been complaining of a headache.

"I . . . do you know . . . I murdered someone."

He said this and smiled, with a face as white as chalk. "Why is it he is smiling?" The thought flashed through my mind before I realised anything else. I too turned pale.

"What are you saying?" I cried.

"You see," he said, with a pale smile, "how much it has cost me to say the first word. Now I have said it, I feel I've taken the first step and shall go on."

For a long while I could not believe him, and I did not believe him at that time, but only after he had been to see me three days running and told me all about it. I thought he was mad, but ended by being convinced, to my great grief and amazement. His crime was a great and terrible one.

Fourteen years before, he had murdered the widow of a landowner, a wealthy and handsome young woman who had a house in our town. He fell passionately in love with her, declared his feeling, and tried to persuade her to marry him. But she had already given her heart to another man, an officer of noble birth and high rank in the service, who was at that time away at the front, though she was expecting him soon to return. She refused his offer and begged him not to come and see her. After he had ceased to visit her, he took advantage of his knowledge of the house to enter at night through the garden by the roof, at great risk of discovery. But as often happens, a crime committed with extraordinary audacity is more successful than others.

Entering the garret through the skylight, he went down the ladder, knowing that the door at the bottom of it was sometimes, through the negligence of the servants, left unlocked. He hoped to find it so, and so it was. He made his way in the dark to her bedroom, where a light was burning. As though on purpose, both her maids had gone off to a birthday party on the same street, without asking leave. The other servants slept in the servants' quarters or in the kitchen on the ground floor. His passion flamed up at the sight of her asleep, and then vindictive, jealous anger took possession of his heart, and like a drunken man, beside himself, he thrust a knife into her heart, so that she did not even cry out. Then with devilish and criminal cunning he contrived that suspicion should fall on the servants. He was so base as to take her purse, to open her chest with keys from under her pillow, and to take some things from it, doing it all as it might have been done by an ignorant servant, leaving valuable papers and taking only money. He took some of the larger gold things, but left smaller articles that were ten times as valuable. He took with him, too, some things for himself as remembrances, but of that later. Having done this awful deed, he returned by the way he had come.

Neither the next day, when the alarm was raised, nor at any time after in his life did anyone dream of suspecting that he was the criminal. No one indeed knew of his love for her, for he was always reserved and silent and had no friend to whom he would have opened his heart. He was looked upon simply as an acquaintance, and not a very intimate one, of the murdered woman, as for the previous fortnight he had not even visited her. A serf of hers called Pyotr was at once suspected, and every circumstance confirmed the suspicion. The man knew—indeed his mistress did not conceal the fact—that having to send one of her serfs as a recruit she had decided to send him, as he had no relations and his conduct was unsatisfactory. People had heard him angrily threatening to murder her when he was drunk in a tavern. Two days before her death, he had run away, staying no one knew where in the town. The day after the murder, he was found on the road leading out of the town, dead drunk, with a knife in his pocket, and his right hand happened to be stained with blood. He declared that his nose had been bleeding, but no one believed him. The maids confessed that they had gone to a party and that the street door had been left open till they returned. And a number of similar details came to light, throwing suspicion on the innocent servant.

They arrested him, and he was tried for the murder; but a week after the arrest, the prisoner fell sick of a fever and died unconscious in the hospital. There the matter ended and the judges and the authorities and everyone in the town remained convinced that the crime had been committed by no one but the servant who had died in the hospital. And after that the punishment began.

My mysterious visitor, now my friend, told me that at first he was not in the least troubled by pangs of conscience. He was miserable a long time, but not for that reason; only from regret that he had killed the woman he loved, that she was no more, that in killing her he had killed his love, while the fire of passion was still in his veins. But of the innocent blood he had shed, of the murder of a fellow creature, he scarcely thought. The thought that his victim might have become the wife of another man was insupportable to him, and so, for a long time, he was convinced in his conscience that he could not have acted otherwise.

At first he was worried at the arrest of the servant, but his illness and death soon set his mind at rest, for the man's death was apparently (so he reflected at the time) not owing to his arrest or his fright, but a chill he had taken on the day he ran away, when he had lain all night dead drunk on the damp ground. The theft of the money and other things troubled him little, for he argued that the theft had not been committed for gain but to avert suspicion. The sum stolen was small, and he shortly afterwards subscribed the whole of it, and much more, towards the funds for maintaining an almshouse in the town. He did this on purpose to set his conscience at rest about the theft, and it's a remarkable fact that for a long time he really was at peace—he told me this himself. He entered then upon a career of great activity in the service, volunteered for a difficult and laborious duty, which occupied him two years, and being a man of strong will almost forgot the past. Whenever he recalled it, he tried not to think of it at all. He became active in philanthropy too, founded and helped to maintain many institutions in the town, did a good deal in the two capitals, and in both Moscow and Petersburg was elected a member of philanthropic societies.

At last, however, he began brooding over the past, and the strain of it was too much for him. Then he was attracted by a fine and intelligent girl and soon after married her, hoping that marriage would dispel his lonely depression, and that by entering on a new life and scrupulously doing his duty to his wife and children, he would escape from old memories altogether. But the very opposite of what he expected happened. He began, even in the first month of his marriage, to be continually fretted by the thought, "My wife loves me—but what if she knew?" When she first told him that she would soon bear him a child, he was troubled. "I am giving life, but I have taken life." Children came. "How dare I love them, teach and educate them, how can I talk to them of virtue? I have shed blood." They were splendid children; he longed to caress them. "And I can't look at their innocent candid faces, I am unworthy."

At last he began to be bitterly and ominously haunted by the blood of his murdered victim, by the young life he had destroyed, by the blood that cried out for vengeance. He had begun to have awful dreams. But being a man of fortitude, he bore his suffering a long time, thinking, "I shall expiate everything by this secret agony." But that hope too was vain; the longer it went on, the more intense was his suffering.

He was respected in society for his active benevolence, though everyone was overawed by his stern and gloomy character. But the more he was respected, the more intolerable it was for him. He confessed to me that he had thoughts of killing himself. But he began to be haunted by another idea—an idea which he had at first regarded as impossible and unthinkable, though at last it got such a hold on his heart that he could not shake it off. He dreamed of rising up, going out, and confessing in the face of all men that he had committed murder. For three years this dream had pursued him, haunting him in different forms. At last he believed with his whole heart that if he confessed his crime, he would heal his soul and would be at peace forever. But this belief filled his heart with terror, for how could he carry it out? And then came what happened at my duel.

"Looking at you, I made up my mind."

I looked at him.

"Is it possible," I cried, clasping my hands, "that such a trivial incident could give rise to such a resolution in you?"

"My resolution has been growing for the last three years," he answered, "and your story only gave the last touch to it. Looking at you,

I reproached myself and envied you." He said this to me almost sullenly.

"But you won't be believed," I observed; "it's fourteen years ago."

"I have proofs, great proofs. I shall show them."

Then I cried and kissed him.

"Tell me one thing, one thing," he said (as though it all depended upon me), "my wife, my children! My wife may die of grief, and though my children won't lose their rank and property, they'll be a convict's children and forever! And what a memory, what a memory of me I shall leave in their hearts!"

I said nothing.

"And to part from them, to leave them forever? It's forever, you know, forever!"

I sat still and repeated a silent prayer. I got up at last, I felt afraid.

"Well?" He looked at me.

"Go!" said I. "Confess. Everything passes; only the truth remains. Your children will understand, when they grow up, the nobility of your resolution."

He left me that time as though he had made up his mind. Yet for more than a fortnight afterwards, he came to me every evening, still preparing himself, still unable to bring himself to the point. He made my heart ache. One day he would come determined and say fervently:

"I know it will be heaven for me, heaven, the moment I confess. Fourteen years I've been in hell. I want to suffer. I will take my punishment and begin to live. You can pass through the world doing wrong, but there's no turning back. Now I dare not love my neighbor nor even my own children. Good God, my children will understand, perhaps, what my punishment has cost me, and will not condemn me! God is not in strength but in truth."

"All will understand your sacrifice," I said to him, "if not at once, they will understand later; for you have served truth, the higher truth, not of the earth."

And he would go away seeming comforted, but the next day he would come again, bitter, pale, sarcastic.

"Every time I come to you, you look at me so inquisitively as though to say, 'He has still not confessed!' Wait a bit, don't despise me too much. It's not such an easy thing to do, as you would think. Perhaps I shall not do it at all. You won't go and inform against me, then, will you?"

And far from looking at him with indiscreet curiosity, I was afraid to look at him at all. I was quite ill from anxiety, and my heart was full of tears. I could not sleep at night.

"I have just come from my wife," he went on. "Do you understand what the word 'wife' means? When I went out, the children called to me, 'Goodbye, father, make haste back to read *The Children's Magazine* with us.' No, you don't understand that! No one is wise from another man's woe."

His eyes were glittering, his lips were twitching. Suddenly he struck the table with his fist so that everything on it danced—it was the first time he had done such a thing, he was such a mild man.

"But need I?" he exclaimed, "must I? No one has been condemned; no one has been sent to Siberia in my place; the man died of fever. And I've been punished by my sufferings for the blood I shed. And I won't be believed; they won't believe my proofs. Need I confess, need I? I am ready to go on suffering all my life for the blood I have shed, if only my wife and children may be spared. Will it be just to ruin them with me? Aren't we making a mistake? What is right in this case? And will people recognize it; will they appreciate it; will they respect it?"

"Good Lord!" I thought to myself, "he is thinking of other people's respect at such a moment!" And I felt so sorry for him then, that I believe I would have shared his fate if it could have comforted him. I saw he was beside himself. I was aghast, realizing with my heart as well as my mind what such a resolution meant.

"Decide my fate!" he exclaimed again.

"Go and confess," I whispered to him. My voice failed me, but I whispered it firmly. I took up the New Testament from the table, the Russian translation, and showed him the Gospel of St. John, chapter 12, verse 24:

"Verily, verily, I say unto you, except a corn of wheat fall into the ground and die, it abideth alone; but if it die, it bringeth forth much fruit."

I had just been reading that verse when he came in. He read it.

"That's true," he said, but he smiled bitterly. "It's terrible the things you find in those books," he said, after a pause. "It's easy enough to thrust them upon one. And who wrote them? Can they have been written by men?"

"The Holy Spirit wrote them," said I.

"It's easy for you to prate," he smiled again, this time almost with hatred.

I took the book again, opened it in another place and showed him the Epistle to the Hebrews, chapter 10, verse 31. He read:

"It is a fearful thing to fall into the hands of the living God."

He read it and simply flung down the book. He was trembling all over.

"An awful text," he said. "There's no denying you've picked out fitting ones." He rose from the chair. "Well!" he said, "Goodbye; perhaps I shan't come again . . . we shall meet in heaven. So I have been for fourteen years 'in the hands of the living God,' that's how one must think of those fourteen years. Tomorrow I will beseech those hands to let me go."

I wanted to take him in my arms and kiss him, but I did not dare—his face was contorted and sombre. He went away.

"Good God," I thought, "what has he gone to face!" I fell on my knees before the icon and wept for him before the Holy Mother of God, our swift defender and helper. I was half an hour praying in tears, and it was late, about midnight. Suddenly I saw the door open and he came in again. I was suprised.

"Where have you been?" I asked him.

"I think," he said, "I've forgotten something . . . my handkerchief, I think. . . . Well, even if I've not forgotten anything, let me stay a little."

He sat down. I stood over him.

"You sit down, too," said he.

I sat down. We sat still for two minutes; he looked intently at me and suddenly smiled—I remembered that—then he got up, embraced me warmly and kissed me.

"Remember," he said, "how I came to you a second time. Do you hear, remember it!"

And he went out.

"Tomorrow," I thought.

And so it was. I did not know that evening that the next day was his birthday. I had not been out for the last few days, so I had no chance of hearing it from anyone. On that day he always had a great gathering; everyone in the town went to it. It was the same this time. After dinner he walked into the middle of the room, with a paper in his hand—a formal declaration to the chief of his department who was present. This declaration he read aloud to the whole assembly. It contained a full account of the crime, in every detail.

"I cut myself off from men as a monster. God has visited me," he said in conclusion. "I want to suffer for my sin!"

Then he brought out and laid on the table all the things he had been keeping for fourteen years that he thought would prove his crime: the jewels belonging to the murdered woman which he had stolen to divert suspicion, a cross and locket taken from her neck with a portrait of her betrothed in the locket, her notebook, and two letters—one from her betrothed, telling her that he would soon be with her, and her unfinished answer left on the table to be sent off the next day. He carried off these two letters—what for? Why had he kept them for fourteen years afterwards instead of destroying them as evidence against him?

And this is what happened: everyone was amazed and horrified, everyone refused to believe it and thought that he was deranged, though all listened with intense curiosity. A few days later it was fully decided and agreed in every house that the unhappy man was mad. The legal authorities could not refuse to take the case up, but they too dropped it. Though the trinkets and letters made them ponder, they decided that even if they did turn out to be authentic, no charge could be based on those alone. Besides, she might have given him those things as a friend, or asked him to take care of them for her. I heard afterwards, however, that the genuineness of the things was proved by the friends and relations of the murdered woman, and that there was no doubt about them. Yet nothing was destined to come of it, after all.

Five days later, all had heard that he was ill and that his life was in danger. The nature of his illness I can't explain; they said it was an affection of the heart. But it became known that the doctors had been induced by his wife to investigate his mental condition also, and had come to the conclusion that it was a case of insanity. I betrayed nothing, though people ran to question me. But when I wanted to visit him, I was for a long while forbidden to do so, above all by his wife. "It's you who have caused his illness," she said to me; "he was always gloomy, but for the last year people noticed that he was peculiarly excited and did strange things, and now you have been the ruin of him. Your preaching has brought him to this; for the last month he was always with you."

Indeed, not only his wife but the whole town were down on me and blamed me. "It's all your doing," they said. I was silent and indeed rejoiced at heart, for I saw plainly God's mercy to the man who had turned against himself and punished himself. I could not believe in his insanity.

They let me see him at last; he insisted upon saying goodbye to me.

I went in to him and saw at once that not only his days, but his hours were numbered. He was weak, yellow; his hands trembled; he gasped for breath, but his face was full of tender and happy feeling.

"It is done!" he said. "I've long been yearning to see you; why didn't you come?"

I did not tell him that they would not let me see him.

"God has had pity on me and is calling me to Himself. I know I am dying, but I feel joy and peace for the first time after so many years. There was heaven in my heart from the moment I had done what I had to do. Now I dare to love my children and to kiss them. Neither my wife nor the judges nor anyone has believed it. My children will never believe it either. I see in that God's mercy to them. I shall die, and my name will be without a stain for them. And now I feel God near, my heart rejoices as in Heaven . . . I have done my duty."

He could not speak; he gasped for breath; he pressed my hand warmly, looking fervently at me. We did not talk for long; his wife kept peeping in at us. But he had time to whisper to me:

"Do you remember how I came back to you that second time, at midnight? I told you to remember it. You know what I came back for? I came to kill you!"

I started.

"I went out from you then into the darkness; I wandered about the streets, struggling with myself. And suddenly I hated you so that I could hardly bear it. Now, I thought, he is all that binds me, and he is my judge. I can't refuse to face my punishment tomorrow, for he knows all. It was not that I was afraid you would betray me (I never even thought of that) but I thought, 'How can I look him in the face if I don't confess?' And if you had been at the other end of the earth, but alive it would have been all the same; the thought was unendurable that you were alive knowing everything and condemning me. I hated you as though you were the cause, as though you were to blame for everything. I came back to you then, remembering that you had a dagger lying on your table. I sat down and asked you to sit down, and for a whole minute I pondered. If I had killed you, I should have been ruined by that murder even if I had not confessed the other. But I didn't think about that at all, and I didn't want to think of it at that moment. I only hated you and longed to revenge myself on you for everything. The Lord vanquished the devil in my heart. But let me tell you, you were never nearer death."

A week later he died. The whole town followed him to the grave.

The chief priest made a speech full of feeling. All lamented the terrible illness that had cut short his days. But all the town was up in arms against me after the funeral, and people even refused to see me. Some, at first a few and afterwards more, began indeed to believe in the truth of his story, and they visited me and questioned me with great interest and eagerness, for man loves to see the downfall and disgrace of the righteous. But I held my tongue, and very shortly after, I left the town, and five months later by God's grace I entered upon the safe and blessed path, praising the unseen finger which had guided me so clearly to it. But I remember in my prayer to this day, the servant of God, Mihail, who suffered so greatly.

CONVERSATIONS AND EXHORTATIONS OF FATHER ZOSSIMA

(e) The Russian monk and his possible significance

Fathers and teachers, what is the monk? In the cultivated world, the word is nowadays pronounced by some people with a jeer, and by others it is used as a term of abuse, and this contempt for the monk is growing. It is true, alas, it is true, that there are many sluggards, gluttons, profligates, and insolent beggars among monks. Educated people point to these: "You are idlers, useless members of society; you live on the labor of others; you are shameless beggars." And yet how many meek and humble monks there are, yearning for solitude and fervent prayer in peace. These are less noticed, or passed over in silence. And how surprised men would be if I were to say that from these meek monks, who yearn for solitary prayer, the salvation of Russia will come perhaps once more. For they are in truth made ready in peace and quiet "for the day and the hour, the month and the year." Meanwhile, in their solitude, they keep the image of Christ fair and undefiled, in the purity of God's truth, from the times of the Fathers of old, the Apostles and the martyrs. And when the time comes, they will show it to the tottering creeds of the world. That is a great thought. That star will rise out of the East.

That is my view of the monk, and is it false? Is it too proud? Look at the worldly and all who set themselves up above the people of God: has not God's image and His truth been distorted in them? They have science; but in science there is nothing but what is the object of sense. The spiritual world, the higher part of man's being, is rejected altogether, dismissed with a sort of triumph, even with hatred. The world has proclaimed the reign of freedom, especially of late, but what do we see in this freedom of theirs? Nothing but slavery and self-destruction! For the world says:

"You have desires and so satisfy them, for you have the same rights as the most rich and powerful. Don't be afraid of satisfying them, and even multiply your desires." That is the modern doctrine of the world. In that they see freedom. And what follows from this right of multi-plication of desires? In the rich, isolation and spiritual suicide; in the poor, envy and murder; for they have been given rights, but have not been shown the means of satisfying their wants. They maintain that the world is getting more and more united, more and more bound together in brotherly community, as it overcomes distance and sets thoughts flying through the air.

Alas, put no faith in such a bond of union. Interpreting freedom as the multiplication and rapid satisfaction of desires, men distort their own nature, for many senseless and foolish desires and habits and ridiculous fancies are fostered in them. They live only for mutual envy, for luxury and ostentation. To have dinners, visits, carriages, rank, and slaves to wait on one is looked upon as a necessity, for which life, honor, and human feeling are sacrificed, and men even commit suicide if they are unable to satisfy it. We see the same thing among those who are not rich, while the poor drown their unsatisfied need and their envy in drunkenness. But soon they will drink blood instead of wine, they are being led on to it. I ask you, is such a man free? I knew one "champion of freedom" who told me himself that, when he was deprived of tobacco in prison, he was so wretched at the privation that he almost went and betrayed his cause for the sake of getting tobacco again! And such a man says, "I am fighting for the cause of humanity."

How can such a one fight; what is he fit for? He is capable perhaps of some action quickly over, but he cannot hold out long. And it's no wonder that instead of gaining freedom, they have sunk into slavery, and instead of serving the cause of brotherly love and the union of humanity, have fallen on the contrary into dissension and isolation, as my mysterious visitor and teacher said to me in my youth. And there-fore the idea of the service of humanity, of brotherly love and the solidarity of mankind, is more and more dying out in the world, and indeed this idea is sometimes treated with derision. For how can a man shake off his habits, what can become of him if he is in such bondage to the habit of satisfying the innumerable desires he has created for himself? He is isolated, and what concern has he with the rest of humanity? They have succeeded in accumulating a greater mass of objects, but the joy in the world has grown less.

The monastic way is very different. Obedience, fasting, and prayer are laughed at, yet only through them lies the way to real, true freedom. I cut off my superfluous and unnecessary desires; I subdue my proud and wanton will and chastise it with obedience, and with God's help I attain freedom of spirit and with it spiritual joy. Which is most capable of conceiving a great idea and serving it—the rich man in his isolation or the man who has freed himself from the tyranny of material things and habits? The monk is reproached for his solitude: "You have secluded yourself within the walls of the monastery for your own salvation, and have forgotten the brotherly service of humanity!" But we shall see which will be most zealous in the cause of brotherly love. For it is not we, but they, who are in isolation, though they don't see that. Of old, leaders of the people came from among us, and why should they not again? The same meek and humble ascetics will rise up and go out to work for the great cause. The salvation of Russia comes from the people. And the Russian monk has always been on the side of the people. We are isolated only if the people are isolated. The people believe as we do, and an unbelieving reformer will never do anything in Russia, even if he is sincere in heart and a genius. Remember that! The people will meet the atheist and overcome him, and Russia will be one and orthodox. Take care of the peasant and guard his heart. Go on educating him quietly. That's your duty as monks, for the peasant has God in his heart.

(f) Of masters and servants, and of whether it is possible for them to be brothers in the spirit

Of course, I don't deny that there is sin in the peasants too. And the fire of corruption is spreading visibly, hourly, working from above downwards. The spirit of isolation is coming upon the people too. Moneylenders and devourers of the commune are rising up. Already the merchant grows more and more eager for rank, and strives to show himself cultured though he has not a trace of culture, and to this end meanly despises his old traditions, and is even ashamed of the faith of his fathers. He visits princes, though he is only a peasant corrupted. The peasants are rotting in drunkenness and cannot shake off the habit. And what cruelty to their wives, to their children even! All from drunkenness! I've seen in the factories children of nine years old, frail, rickety, bent, and already depraved. The stuffy workshop, the din of machinery, work all day long, the vile language and the drink, the drink—is that what a little child's heart needs? He needs sunshine, childish play, good examples all about him, and at least a little love. There must be no more of this, monks, no more torturing of children; rise up and preach that, make haste, make haste!

But God will save Russia, for though the peasants are corrupted and cannot renounce their filthy sin, yet they know it is cursed by God and that they do wrong in sinning. So that our people still believe in righteousness, have faith in God, and weep tears of devotion.

It is different with the upper classes. They, following science, want to base justice on reason alone, not with Christ, as before, and they have already proclaimed that there is no crime, that there is no sin. And that's consistent, for if you have no God, what is the meaning of crime? In Europe, the people are already rising up against the rich with violence, and the leaders of the people are everywhere leading them to bloodshed, and teaching them that their wrath is righteous. But their "wrath is accursed, for it is cruel." But God will save Russia as He has saved her many times. Salvation will come from the people, from their faith and their meekness.

Fathers and teachers, watch over the people's faith and this will not be a dream. I've been struck all my life in our great people by their dignity, their true and seemly dignity. I've seen it myself, I can testify to it, I've seen it and marvelled at it; I've seen it in spite of the degraded sins and poverty-stricken appearance of our peasantry. They are not servile, and even after two centuries of serfdom, they are free in manner and bearing, yet without insolence, and not revengeful and not envious. "You are rich and noble; you are clever and talented; well be so, God bless you. I respect you, but I know that I too am a man. By the very fact that I respect you without envy, I prove my dignity as a man."

In truth if they don't say this (for they don't know how to say this yet), that is how they act. I have seen it myself, I have known it myself, and, would you believe it, the poorer our Russian peasant is, the more noticeable is that serene goodness, for the rich among them are for the most part corrupted already, and much of that is due to our carelessness and indifference. But God will save His people, for Russia is great in her humility. I dream of seeing, and seem to see clearly already, our future. It will come to pass that even the most corrupt of our rich will end by being ashamed of his riches before the poor, and the poor, seeing his humility, will understand and give way before him—will respond joyfully and kindly to his honorable shame. Believe me that it will end in that; things are moving to that. Equality is to be found only in the spiritual dignity of man, and that will only be understood among us. If we were brothers, there would be fraternity, but before that, they will never agree about the division of wealth. We preserve the image of Christ, and it will shine forth like a precious diamond to the whole world. So may it be, so may it be!

Fathers and teachers, a touching incident befell me once. In my wanderings I met in the town of K. my old orderly, Afanasy. It was eight years since I had parted from him. He chanced to see me in the marketplace, recognized me, ran up to me, and how delighted he was; he simply pounced on me: "Master dear, is it you? is it really you I see?" He took me home with him.

He was no longer in the army; he was married and already had two little children. He and his wife earned their living as vendors in the marketplace. His room was poor, but bright and clean. He made me sit down, set the samovar, and sent for his wife, as though my appearance were a festival for them. He brought me his children: "Bless them, father."

"Is it for me to bless them? I am only a humble monk. I will pray for them. And for you, Afanasy Pavlovich, I have prayed every day since that day, for it all came from you," said I. And I explained that to him as well as I could. And what do you think? The man kept gazing at me and could not believe that I, his former master, an officer, was now before him in such a guise and position; it made him shed tears.

"Why are you weeping?" said I. "Better rejoice over me, dear friend, whom I can never forget, for my path is a glad and joyful one."

He did not say much, but kept sighing and shaking his head over me tenderly.

"What has become of your fortune?" he asked.

"I gave it to the monastery," I answered. "We live in common."

After tea, I began saying goodbye, and suddenly he brought out half a ruble as an offering to the monastery, and another half-ruble I saw him thrusting hurriedly into my hand: "That's for you in your wanderings; it may be of use to you, father."

I took his half-ruble, bowed to him and his wife, and went out rejoicing. And on my way I thought, "Here we are both now, he at home and I on the road, sighing and shaking our heads no doubt, and yet smiling joyfully in the gladness of our hearts, remembering how God brought about our meeting."

I have never seen him again since then. I had been his master and he my servant, but now when we exchanged a loving kiss with softened hearts, there was a great human bond between us. I have thought a great deal about that, and now what I think is this. Is it so inconceivable that that grand and simple-hearted unity might in due time become universal among the Russian people? I believe that it will come to pass, and that the time is at hand.

And of servants I will add this: in olden days when I was young I was often angry with servants: "The cook had served something too hot, the orderly had not brushed my clothes." But what taught me better then was a thought of my dear brother's, which I had heard from him in childhood: "Am I worth it, that another should serve me and be ordered about by me in his poverty and ignorance?" And I wondered at the time that such simple and self-evident ideas should be so slow to occur to our minds.

It is impossible that there should be no servants in the world, but act so that your servant may be freer in spirit than if he were not a servant. And why cannot I be a servant to my servant and even let him see it, and that without any pride on my part or any mistrust on his? Why should not my servant be like my own kindred, so that I may take him into my family and rejoice in doing so? Even now this can be done, but it will lead to the grand unity of men in the future, when a man will not seek servants for himself, or desire to turn his fellow creatures into servants as he does now, but on the contrary will long with his whole heart to be the servant of all, as the Gospel teaches.

And can it be a dream, that in the end man will find his joy only in deeds of light and mercy, and not in cruel pleasures as now: in gluttony, fornication, ostentation, boasting, and envious rivalry of one with the other? I firmly believe that it is not, and that the time is at hand. People laugh and ask, "When will that time come, and does it look like it is coming?" I believe that with Christ's help we shall accomplish this great thing. And how many ideas there have been on earth in the history of man which were unthinkable ten years before they appeared? Yet when their destined hour had come, they came forth and spread over the whole earth. So it will be with us, and our people will shine forth in the world, and all men will say: "The stone which the builders rejected has become the cornerstone of the building."

And may we ask the scornful themselves: if our hope is a dream, when will you build up your edifice and order things justly by your intellect alone, without Christ? If they declare that it is they who are advancing towards unity, only the most simple-hearted among them believe it, so that one may positively marvel at such simplicity. Of a truth, they have more fantastic dreams than we. They aim at justice but, denying Christ, they will end by flooding the earth with blood, for blood cries out for blood, and he that taketh up the sword shall perish by the sword. And if it were not for Christ's covenant, they would slaughter one another down to the last two men on earth. And those two last men would not be able to restrain each other in their pride, and the one would slay the other and then himself. And that would come to pass, were it not for the promise of Christ that for the sake of the humble and meek the days shall be shortened.

While I was still wearing an officer's uniform after my duel, I talked about servants in general society, and I remember everyone was amazed at me. "What!" they asked, "are we to make our servants sit down on the sofa and offer them tea?" And I answered them, "Why not, sometimes at least." Everyone laughed. Their question was frivolous and my answer was not clear; but the thought in it was to some extent right.

(g) Of prayer, of love, and of contact with other worlds

Young man, be not forgetful of prayer. Every time you pray, if your prayer is sincere, there will be new feeling and new meaning in it, which will give you fresh courage, and you will understand that prayer is an education. Remember, too, every day, and whenever you can, repeat to yourself, "Lord, have mercy on all who appear before Thee today." For every hour and every moment thousands of men leave life on this earth, and their souls appear before God. And how many of them depart in solitude, unknown, sad, dejected, that no one mourns for them or even knows whether they have lived or not. And behold, from the other end of the earth perhaps, your prayer for their rest will rise up to God, though you knew them not nor they you. How touching it must be to a soul standing in dread before the Lord to feel at that instant that, for him too, there is one to pray, that there is a fellow creature left on earth to love him too. And God will look on you both more graciously, for if you have had so much pity on him, how much more will He have pity Who is infinitely more loving and merciful than you. And He will forgive him for your sake.

Brothers, have no fear of men's sin. Love a man even in his sin, for that is the semblance of Divine Love and is the highest love on earth. Love all God's creation, the whole and every grain of sand in it. Love every leaf, every ray of God's light. Love the animals; love the plants; love everything. If you love everything, you will perceive the divine mystery in things. Once you perceive it, you will begin to comprehend it better every day. And you will come at last to love the whole world with an all-embracing love. Love the animals: God has given them the rudiments of thought and joy untroubled. Do not trouble them; don't harass them; don't deprive them of their happiness; don't work against God's intent. Man, do not pride yourself on superiority to the animals; they are without sin, and you, with your greatness, defile the earth by your appearance on it, and leave the traces of your foulness after you— alas, it is true of almost every one of us! Love children especially, for they too are sinless like the angels; they live to soften and purify our hearts and as it were to guide us. Woe to him who offends a child! Father Anfim taught me to love children. The kind, silent man used often on our wanderings to spend the coins given us on sweets and cakes for the children. He could not pass by a child without emotion, that's the nature of the man.

At some thoughts one stands perplexed, especially at the sight of men's sin, and wonders whether one should use force or humble love. Always decide to use humble love. If you resolve on that once for all, you may subdue the whole world. Loving humility is marvellously strong, the strongest of all things, and there is nothing else like it.

Every day and every hour, every minute, walk round yourself and watch yourself, and see that your image is a seemly one. You pass by a little child, you pass by, spiteful, with ugly words, with wrathful heart; you may not have noticed the child, but he has seen you, and your image, unseemly and ignoble, may remain in his defenceless heart. You don't know it, but you may have sown an evil seed in him and it may grow, and all because you were not careful before the child, because you did not foster in yourself a careful, actively benevolent love. Brothers, love is a teacher; but one must know how to acquire it, for it is hard to acquire; it is dearly bought; it is won slowly by long labor. For we must love not only occasionally, for a moment, but forever. Everyone can love occasionally; even the wicked can.

My brother asked the birds to forgive him; that sounds senseless, but it is right; for all is like an ocean, all is flowing and blending; a touch in one place sets up movement at the other end of the earth. It may be senseless to beg forgiveness of the birds, but birds would be happier at your side—a little happier, anyway—and children and all animals, if you yourself were nobler than you are now. It's all like an ocean, I tell you. Then you would pray to the birds too, consumed by an all-embracing love, in a sort of transport, and pray that they too will forgive you your sin. Treasure this ecstasy, however senseless it may seem to men.

My friends, pray to God for gladness. Be glad as children, as the birds of heaven. And let not the sin of men confound you in your doings. Fear not that it will wear away your work and hinder its being accomplished. Do not say, "Sin is mighty, wickedness is mighty, evil environment is mighty, and we are lonely and helpless, and evil environment is wearing us away and hindering our good work from being done." Fly from that dejection, children! There is only one means of salvation, then: take yourself and make yourself responsible for all men's sins; that is the truth, you know, friends, for as soon as you sincerely make yourself responsible for everything and for all men, you will see at once that it is really so, and that you are to blame for everyone and for all things. But throwing your own indolence and impotence on others, you will end by sharing the pride of Satan and murmuring against God.

Of the pride of Satan what I think is this: it is hard for us on earth to comprehend it, and therefore it is so easy to fall into error and to share it, even imagining that we are doing something grand and fine. Indeed many of the strongest feelings and movements of our nature we cannot comprehend on earth. Let not that be a stumbling block, and think not that it may serve as a justification to you for anything. For the Eternal Judge asks of you what you can comprehend and not what you cannot. You will know that yourself hereafter, for you will behold all things truly then and will not dispute them. On earth, indeed, we are as it were astray, and if it were not for the precious image of Christ before us, we should be undone and altogether lost, as was the human race before the flood. Much on earth is hidden from us, but to make up for that we have been given a precious mystic sense of our living bond with the other world, with the higher heavenly world, and the roots of our thoughts and feelings are not here but in other worlds. That is why the philosophers say that we cannot apprehend the reality of things on earth.

God took seeds from different worlds and sowed them on this earth, and His garden grew up and everything came up that could come up, but what grows lives and is alive only through the feeling of its contact with other mysterious worlds. If that feeling grows weak or is destroyed in you, the heavenly growth will die away in you. Then you will be indifferent to life and even grow to hate it. That's what I think.

(h) Can a man judge his fellow creature? Faith to the end

Remember particularly that you cannot be a judge of anyone. For no one can judge a criminal, until he recognizes that he is just such a criminal as the man standing before him, and that he perhaps is more than all men to blame for that crime. When he understands that, he will be able to be a judge. Though that sounds absurd, it is true. If I had been righteous myself, perhaps there would have been no criminal standing before me. If you can take upon yourself the crime of the criminal your heart is judging, take it at once, suffer for him yourself, and let him go without reproach. And even if the law itself makes you his judge, act in the same spirit so far as possible, for he will go away and condemn himself more bitterly than you have done. If, after your kiss, he goes away untouched, mocking at you, do not let that be a stumbling block to you. It shows his time has not yet come, but it will come in due course. And if it does not come, no matter; if not he, then another in his place will understand and suffer, and judge and condemn himself, and the truth will be fulfilled. Believe that, believe it without doubt; for in that lies all the hope and faith of the saints.

Work without ceasing. If you remember in the night as you go to sleep, "I have not done what I ought to have done," rise up at once and do it. If the people around you are spiteful and callous and will not hear you, fall down before them and beg their forgiveness; for in truth you are to blame for their not wanting to hear you. And if you cannot speak to them in their bitterness, serve them in silence and in humility, never losing hope. If all men abandon you and even drive you away by force, then when you are left alone fall on the earth and kiss it, water it with your tears and it will bring forth fruit even though no one has seen or heard you in your solitude. Believe to the end, even if all men went astray and you were left the only one faithful; bring your offering even then and praise God in your loneliness. And if two of you are gathered together—then there is a whole world, a world of living love. Embrace each other tenderly and praise God, for if only in you two His truth has been fulfilled.

If you sin yourself and grieve even unto death for your sins or for your sudden sin, then rejoice for others, rejoice in the righteous man, rejoice that if you have sinned, he is righteous and has not sinned.

If the evildoing of men moves you to indignation and overwhelming distress, even to a desire for vengeance on the evildoers, shun above all things that feeling. Go at once and seek suffering for yourself, as though you were yourself guilty of that wrong. Accept that suffering and bear it, and your heart will find comfort, and you will understand that you too are guilty, for you might have been a light to the evildoers, even as the one man sinless, and you were not a light to them. If you had been a light, you would have lightened the path for others too, and the evildoer might perhaps have been saved by your light from his sin. And even though your light was shining, yet you see men were not saved by it; hold firm and doubt not the power of the heavenly light. Believe that if they were not saved, they will be saved hereafter. And if they are not saved hereafter, then their sons will be saved, for your light will not die even when you are dead. The righteous man departs, but his light remains. Men are always saved after the death of the deliverer. Men reject their prophets and slay them, but they love their martyrs and honor those whom they have slain. You are working for the whole, you are acting for the future. Seek no reward, for great is your reward on this earth: the spiritual joy which is only vouchsafed to the righteous man. Fear not the great nor the mighty, but be wise and ever serene. Know the measure; know the times; study that. When you are left alone, pray. Love to throw yourself on the earth and kiss it. Kiss the earth and love it with an unceasing, consuming love. Love all men; love everything. Seek that rapture and ecstasy. Water the earth with the tears of your joy and love those tears. Don't be ashamed of that ecstasy; prize it, for it is a gift of God and a great one; it is not given to many but only to the elect.

(i) Of hell and hell fire, a mystic reflection

Fathers and teachers, I ponder "What is hell?" I maintain that it is the suffering of being unable to love. Once in infinite existence, immeasurable in time and space, a spiritual creature was given on his coming to earth, the power of saying, "I am and I love." Once, only once, there was given him a moment of active *living* love, and for that was earthly life given him, and with it times and seasons. And that happy creature rejected the priceless gift, prized it and loved it not, scorned it and remained callous. Such a one, having left the earth, sees Abraham's bosom and talks with Abraham as we are told in the parable of the rich man and Lazarus, and beholds heaven and can go up to the Lord. But that is just his torment, to rise up to the Lord without ever having loved, to be brought close to those who have loved when he has despised their love. For he sees clearly and says to himself, "Now I have understanding, and though I now thirst to love, there will be nothing great, no sacrifice in my love, for my earthly life is over, and Abraham will not come even with a drop of living water (that is, the gift of earthly, active life) to cool the fiery thirst of spiritual love which burns in me now, though I despised it on earth; there is no more life for me and will be no more time! Even though I would gladly give my life for others, it can never be, for that life is passed which can be sacrificed for love, and now there is a gulf fixed between that life and this existence."

They talk of hellfire in the material sense. I don't go into that mystery and I shun it. But I think if there were fire in the material sense, they would be glad of it, for I imagine that in material agony their still greater spiritual agony would be forgotten for a moment. Moreover, that spiritual agony cannot be taken from them, for that suffering is not external but within them. And if it could be taken from them, I think it would be bitterer still for the unhappy creatures. For even if the righteous in Paradise forgave them, beholding their torments, and called them up to heaven in their infinite love, they would only multiply their torments, for they would arouse in them still more keenly a flaming thirst for responsive, active, and grateful love, which is now impossible. In the timidity of my heart I imagine, however, that the very recognition of this impossibility would serve at last to console them. For accepting the love of the righteous together with the impossibility of repaying it, by this submissiveness and the effect of this humility, they will attain at last, as it were, to a certain semblance of that active love which they scorned in life, to something like its outward expression . . . I am sorry, friends and brothers, that I cannot express this clearly. But woe to those who have slain themselves on earth, woe to the suicides! I believe that there can be none more miserable than they. They tell us that it is a sin to pray for them and outwardly the Church, as it were, renounces them, but in my secret heart I believe that we may pray even for them. Love can never be an offence to Christ. For such as those I have prayed inwardly all my life; I confess it, fathers and teachers, and even now I pray for them every day.

Oh, there are some who remain proud and fierce even in hell, in spite of their certain knowledge and contemplation of the absolute truth; there are some fearful ones who have given themselves over to Satan and his proud spirit entirely. For such, hell is voluntary and ever consuming; they are tortured by their own choice. For they have cursed themselves, cursing God and life. They live upon their vindictive pride like a starving man in the desert sucking blood out of his own body. But they are never satisfied, and they refuse forgiveness; they curse God Who calls them. They cannot behold the living God without hatred, and they cry out that the God of life should be annihilated, that God should destroy Himself and His own creation. And they will burn in the fire of their own wrath forever and yearn for death and annihilation. But they will not attain to death. . . .